THE MYSTERIOUS MR. SPINES
FLIGHT

By Jason Lethcoe

Cover illustration by Scott Altmann

Grosset & Dunlap

GROSSET & DUNLAP

Published by the Penguin Group
Penguin Group (USA) Inc., 375 Hudson Street,
New York, New York 10014, USA
Penguin Group (Canada), 90 Eglinton Avenue East,
Suite 700, Toronto, Ontario M4P 2Y3, Canada
(a division of Pearson Penguin Canada Inc.)
Penguin Books Ltd., 80 Strand, London WC2R 0RL, England
Penguin Group Ireland, 25 St. Stephen's Green, Dublin 2, Ireland
(a division of Penguin Books Ltd.)
Penguin Group (Australia), 250 Camberwell Road,
Camberwell, Victoria 3124, Australia
(a division of Pearson Australia Group Pty. Ltd.)
Penguin Books India Pvt. Ltd., 11 Community Centre,
Panchsheel Park, New Delhi—110 017, India
Penguin Group (NZ), 67 Apollo Drive, Rosedale, North Shore 0632,
New Zealand (a division of Pearson New Zealand Ltd.)
Penguin Books (South Africa) (Pty.) Ltd., 24 Sturdee Avenue,
Rosebank, Johannesburg 2196, South Africa

Penguin Books Ltd., Registered Offices:
80 Strand, London WC2R 0RL, England

Library of Congress Control Number: 2009006095

ISBN 978-0-448-44885-5   10 9 8 7 6 5 4 3 2 1

For my brother Jeff.

✦   ✦   ✦

A special thank you to Bob Rosen.

If there are indeed two of you in this universe,

then it is a better place for it.

"Tell me, Melchior,

what was it you hoped to achieve by falling?

You knew the consequences.

Why did you do it?"

asked the Elder.

"For me, it was better to fall

and understand love," Melchior replied,

"than to forever wonder."

-An excerpt from the Chronicle of Melchior, W.R. 2675

TABLE OF CONTENTS

✦ Chapter One ✦
CARDS

Edward Macleod reached into his pocket and removed a tattered deck of playing cards. His long fingers twitched, anxious to begin their favorite activity. He needed something to distract him, something to occupy his mind. He was still trying to process everything that had happened to him in the last twenty-four hours. His former life in Portland, Oregon, was long gone, and if he thought too much about it, he felt like he would explode from barely contained excitement.

After shaking the cards loose from the box, he smoothed a wide area on the wooden desk with the edge of his palm. Then, after taking a deep breath, he began stacking the cards with mechanical precision, balancing them on top of each other and allowing a pattern to emerge.

With each card he placed, he felt more and more relaxed. His one-of-a-kind deck of cards was his most precious possession, a gift from his mother when he was very young. She'd been amazed at the elaborate card houses he could build. And for Edward, now an incredibly tall, skinny fourteen-year-old with a stutter, it was the one thing that relaxed him and gave him confidence. It was the only thing that he had ever been truly "good" at.

Edward had seen many playing cards since then, but he didn't think any of them rivaled his deck. The face cards had unusually elaborate portraits of kings, queens, and jacks. And the pips on the numbered cards were different from normal cards. They had real shovels for "spades," gems for "diamonds," and realistic hearts for "hearts." Even the "clubs" were different. Instead of the typical clovers found on most cards, they had wicked looking fighting sticks—real clubs! For Edward, the tattered box was filled not with cards, but with fifty-two familiar friends. And they were the best cards for building houses he'd ever seen.

Edward smiled as he formed the cards into a pattern, never pausing to think about what he was actually building, but allowing the structure to take shape of its own accord.

He drew a card from the stack. The jack of spades was covered in rusted armor. His battered shovel was raised protectively, attempting to fend off a flying dragon. The dragon's recently shed skin lay in a crumpled heap at the bottom of the picture.

Edward glanced from the card to his reflection in the mirror above his bed. He felt a little like he had shed his skin, too. He gazed at his unusually tall, sticklike proportions, and his thatch of messy, black hair. It was the same image he'd seen every day of his life except for one major change. He flexed his shoulders beneath his cable-knit sweater and his brand-new, huge, ebony wings responded with a gentle flap.

He grinned. Just two days ago, what had started as an annoying itch between his shoulders that he couldn't scratch had magically turned into something else . . . something he would have never believed possible!

He'd sprouted wings!

Being careful not to flap them hard enough
to blow his cards over, he resumed building.
The card structure was taking shape beneath
his deft fingers. Triangular supports appeared
like trestles on a railroad bridge. His hands
automatically placed each card in just the right
place, knowing instinctively how to make the
structure as solid as possible. He delicately
positioned the ace of spades—a black shovel with
a grinning skull—on top of the two of clubs.

The creepy-looking ace made him think
of the mysterious Mr. Spines. The stumpy,
porcupine-like man had found him trapped
in the cellar of his terrible boarding school,
and had rescued him from Whiplash Scruggs,
a horribly evil teacher who had tried to cut off
his new wings. After that harrowing incident,
he had learned that Scruggs wasn't really a
man at all, but actually a monster in disguise.
Edward shuddered, and the movement sent
waves rippling through his ebony feathers. He
had barely escaped with his life! But at the last
minute, Edward used Mr. Spines's incredible

machinery to transport himself here, to the Afterlife, a place the locals called the Woodbine.

Until recently, Edward had never known what happened to people when they died. When he'd lost his mother two years ago, he'd thought she'd left him forever. And life had become so miserable after her passing that he'd never even paused to consider that he might be wrong, that she might still exist in another world.

But after arriving here, Edward met Jack the faun and his niece, a pretty redhead named Bridgette. To his amazement, they knew who his mother was and informed him that she was known to the residents as a great warrior called the Blue Lady. Edward would never have believed it if they hadn't shown him a painting of her. In the picture, she was riding a flying horse and carrying a long, silver spear. Since then, she had been caught by Groundlings and imprisoned by an evil being known as the Jackal.

The thought that he could actually find her and see her beautiful, loving face again filled him with hope. He didn't care how impossible Jack and Bridgette had said it would be for him to break into the Jackal's lair. He would face anything if it meant he could see his mother again.

Lost in thought, Edward was just about to place the last card on top of the bridge when the door behind him flew open, sending a forceful gust into the tiny room.

"Hi, Edward." Bridgette stood in the doorway, looking excited. But her face fell as she watched Edward's delicate card house collapse onto the floor. "Oops!"

He smiled and shrugged. "I-It's okay," he stuttered.

"I'm really sorry," she said softly, gazing at the messy pile of cards. "Whatever you were building looked amazing!" She smiled, and Edward could feel his cheeks turning red.

None of the girls at his former school had ever been as nice as Bridgette. They'd spent most of their time teasing him about his unusual height, calling him names like "Bean Pole" and "Sticks" behind his back. It was nice to have a friend. Trying not to show how nervous he still was around her, Edward busied himself by

replacing the scattered cards inside the worn box.
Bridgette walked over and helped gather them up.

"Uncle Jack sent me to tell you that the
meeting is about to begin," she said. Her slim
hand brushed his own as she passed him a few
of the cards. Feeling self-conscious, he quickly
placed the cards inside the box with the others.

"G-great," he said. "I cuh-can't wait to
h-hear what they're going to say."

Last night, after he arrived in the Woodbine,
Jack had hinted that Edward's arrival was
auspicious, that there was something very special
about him. The faun was a respected authority
in Woodbine lore and wanted to gather some
important people to discuss the event. Edward
was very interested to hear what he had to say.

He followed Bridgette downstairs, walking
past a hall filled with odd-looking portraits.
There were several noble-looking fauns, a
double-headed lion, and something that Edward
felt sure was a typewriter with legs. He chuckled
as he descended the twisting stairs, remembering
what Bridgette had told him. Here in the
Woodbine, people were allowed to change their

appearance into something that they thought best resembled their "inner" self. And judging from some of the unusual creatures he'd met so far, the possibilities were endless. He glanced at Bridgette's copper colored hair as she bounded down the stairs in front of him, wondering if she had changed her appearance. It was a curious thought. Had she always been pretty? What had she looked like when she was back on Earth?

He decided that it didn't matter. The only Bridgette he knew was the one he'd met here in the Woodbine. Whoever she'd been back on Earth was in the past. The Woodbine was a clean slate, a second chance for everyone to become the person they'd always hoped to be. He just hoped that was true for him as well.

Smiling, he approached the downstairs common room, noticing that the murmurs of cheerful conversation grew louder and the smell of baking scones filled the air. Edward's stomach rumbled and he smiled happily. He could hardly wait for the meeting to start!

Chapter Two

MEETING

Outside the cottage, thunder rumbled in
the distance, and shortly after, the sound of a
gentle rain pattered down on the thatched roof.
Edward stared out of a nearby window, watching
gray clouds hover over the pine-covered hills.
If he didn't know he was in the Afterlife, he
would have sworn he was in the woods outside
Portland.

Edward pulled his eyes away from the view
and looked around the room. He and Bridgette
were settled on a sofa next to the crackling
fire. He smiled awkwardly at a pair of majestic
Guardians, winged beings like himself, who
were staring at him from the opposite couch.

"H-h-hello," Edward said. The Guardians
smiled back tensely and then resumed their
low conversation. Edward felt embarrassed and

immediately wished he hadn't spoken. He always felt so stupid when he stuttered like that!

Bridgette's uncle Jack sat next to the fire holding a big, leather book. He had been a respected English professor back on Earth, but in the Woodbine he had chosen the appearance of a faun wearing a tweed coat and smoking a pipe. In spite of having goat legs, the clothes suited him in a way Edward couldn't explain. He looked like a teacher or a historian.

Bridgette's aunt Joyce, who was a faun like her husband, was perched on the chair next to Jack. And on the couch across from Edward, next to the two winged Guardians, was a little man with huge, hairy feet.

Edward sighed happily. Now that he was here, Edward's former life in Portland, Oregon, seemed like a bad nightmare. This new life was looking much better so far, although, as usual, he felt a little awkward around all of these people that he didn't really know. But Edward really wanted to make a good impression on everyone he was meeting in the Woodbine, so he was fighting his unease as best he could.

"Hey, look. Tollers is snoring," Bridgette whispered to him.

Edward looked, and the tiny man with exceptionally large, furry feet was indeed snoring gently with his head resting right on the shoulder of the young Guardian next to him. Tollers had helped rescue Edward when he'd fallen in the river the previous evening and was supposed to be an expert in Guardian history.

Bridgette tried to suppress a giggle as Tollers snorted loudly and rolled over. Soon Edward was grinning, too. It was hard not to laugh. The tiny man was completely oblivious to the two Guardians, very honored guests, who were politely pretending not to notice his steady stream of snores and groans.

The larger of the two Guardians was a burly, fierce-looking man with brown skin and gigantic, silver wings. He wore heavy, studded armor and carried a large, curved sword at his side. He was speaking quietly with the younger Guardian next to him. Edward guessed that the girl, who had close-cropped hair and perfectly groomed, pearly pink wings, wasn't much older than he was. Around her waist was a brilliant blue sash, complementing her sturdy, leather coat and trousers.

Bridgette noticed him staring at her and whispered, "Her name's Tabitha and she's one of the best fliers in the Afterlife."

Edward glanced back at his own wings and sighed, noticing how bedraggled they looked. *She probably thinks I look like a molting vulture,* he thought, trying to smooth down his feathers without anyone noticing.

"Would you like some tea, Edward, dear?"

Edward jumped, and glanced up to the plump, little faun who had spoken.

"Th-thank you, Joyce," Edward said with a smile, taking the cup that was offered and trying, as always, not to stutter.

The happy chatter died down as everyone received his or her tea.

Jack cleared his throat, ready to officially begin the meeting, and gave the still sleeping Tollers a shake.

"Wake up, Mr. Tollers," Tabitha said kindly. The Guardian shook his shoulder but the tiny man wouldn't wake up. She tried again, shaking him a little harder. Tollers mumbled something in his sleep about cherry tarts and then snuggled up even closer to Tabitha. Edward and Bridgette couldn't help but laugh.

Tabitha's wings twitched in annoyance and she looked at Jemial for help. The big Guardian shook his head and shrugged. Tabitha looked around helplessly for a moment, and then spotted a nearby poker. She grabbed it and with a swift, deliberate motion, prodded the little man's backside.

Tollers sat up with a loud "Whoop!" The entire room burst into fits of giggles. Tollers glanced around disoriented.

"I wasn't sleeping!" he protested loudly. "I was just resting my eyes!"

As the little man repositioned himself on the sofa, Edward heard him mutter something in a surly voice about young Guardians having a "lack of manners" and "no respect for elders."

Jack waved for silence, chuckling a bit himself, then said, "Let me begin by saying thank you, especially to Guardian Jemial and his apprentice, Tabitha, for joining us on such short notice. I know you're both very busy with duties from the Council and your presence here is greatly appreciated. I think you'll find that what I have to share with you will be of tremendous importance. If what Tollers and I suspect is true, then the future of the Woodbine could be changed forever."

"I'm happy to oblige, Jack," Jemial said in a deep, resonant voice. "You and Tollers are respected authorities in Woodbine lore. The Council is always interested in your findings." As he spoke, the big Guardian glanced at a golden dial affixed to his broad, leather belt. His wings twitched. "But unfortunately, we can't stay long. Tabitha and I are due back in Estrella two hours from now."

"It's my graduation day," Tabitha explained. "I'm being promoted to Guardian Third Class and have been assigned to a flying squadron." Edward noticed that she was fingering a large, golden ring tied to her belt, turning it round and round impatiently.

A chorus of excited voices greeted her

announcement. Everyone in the room offered his or her congratulations. To Tabitha's surprise, Joyce rushed over and threw her arms around her, giving her a big hug. From the expression on her face, Edward could tell that Guardians weren't used to such overt displays of affection. However, Tabitha couldn't help but return the little faun's embrace, patting her lightly on her back and smiling broadly.

"Well, I promise not to keep you long. What I have to say will only take a few minutes," Jack said, interrupting the happy chatter. As the faun turned his attention to the book on his lap, Edward couldn't help wondering what kind of training it took to become a full-fledged Guardian. Were the studies difficult? How hard was it to learn how to fly? Although he had sprouted wings, he had no idea how to use them. He wished someone would offer to train him.

His thoughts were interrupted as Jack turned to a page that was marked by a red ribbon, and handed the large volume to Tollers.

The faun took a quick puff on his pipe and said, "I don't know how many of you are familiar with the *Fall of Melchior*. Until yesterday, Tollers and I considered it one of the more obscure texts in the *Libram Occasum*. The report that is listed there is brief. But after discovering a bit of new information, we felt that a public reading was necessary." He turned to the little man. "If you would, Tollers."

The gray-haired hobbit wiggled his furry toes and lowered his half-moon spectacles. "This report was filed approximately fifteen years ago by a clerk in the Fallen Guardian Records office. The fact that Jack and I spotted it during our research was quite remarkable. Most of the more prominent cases are several pages long. This one, however, is only a paragraph or two. Apparently it wasn't considered of great importance at the time and was recorded in a rather abbreviated fashion."

Edward listened with rapt attention as the little man cleared his throat and glanced down at the page. Moments later his high, clear voice filled the room as he began to read.

"*Let all hear and beware the case of Melchior Hazshaferah, Guardian First Class . . .*"

Chapter Three

REPORT

"Melchior Hazshaferah was considered by many to be the greatest craftsman the Woodbine had ever seen. He created Instruments of Power, Guardian weapons that were filled with powerful magic. Who among us can't recall the Harp of Longing or the Trumpet of Grave Summoning? Both of these instruments currently occupy places of honor inside the Hall of Master Craftings in the Woodbine capital city of Estrella.

Unfortunately, Melchior is no longer a resident of the Woodbine. The Council hasn't released the details of the case, but a spokesman in Estrella confirmed reports that he violated Code 1737, 'Inappropriate Contact with a Mortal.' It is believed that Melchior Hazshaferah enlisted the help of the Jackal and has traded immortality for a mortal body. He's accused of

marrying the mortal woman he was sent to guard,
and was last spotted somewhere in the northwest
region of the United States. The Council has
stated that Melchior has been officially declared a
Groundling Fourth Class and is denied all access
to Guardian Territory. Let all residents of the
Woodbine hear and beware this terrible crime."
-Entry prepared by Jebrial Bethesda,
Records Clerk, W.R. 13.2. 2657

"Thank you, Tollers. If you don't mind, I'd
like to proceed from here," Jack said. Tollers
nodded and closed the large tome.

The report had been brief and somewhat
interesting, but had left Edward feeling
confused. What did it have to do with him?

Jack lit his pipe and took a deep breath.
"Up until recently, Melchior's story has been
overlooked by most scholars. His crime was
considered of little consequence in the general
history of the Woodbine. But yesterday we found
out that there was more to the tale. We've learned
that the relationship Melchior had with the
mortal woman was short-lived, because the evil

power of the Jackal's Corruption began to take its toll."

"I'm sorry, Uncle Jack," Bridgette interrupted, "but would you mind explaining more about the Corruption? I mean, I thought it was a sickness that only fallen Guardians could get. Can humans get it, too?"

The faun paused thoughtfully. "No, Bridgette, humans can't get the Corruption. It's something reserved for fallen Guardians alone. Ever since the Jackal fell, he's used his dark power against any fallen Guardian who resists serving him. The Corruption is a special curse that causes the Guardian to become a twisted, monstrous creature. Their ability to resist the Jackal weakens as they change, and they soon become as evil as their master. Their only thought is to serve him and spread destruction wherever they go. And, of course, like all fallen Guardians, they gradually lose the ability to fly."

Tabitha gasped softly. Edward noticed that she tucked her beautiful wings protectively behind her. He glanced back at his own and gulped. Even if he didn't know how to use his wings yet, the thought of losing them was terrible. They were part of him now, just as real and permanent as his arms or legs.

The faun cleared his throat and said, "In Melchior's case, he recklessly signed a contract with the Jackal when he fell, stating that he was willing to give anything to be with the mortal woman. But he didn't understand fully what she would have to pay for that to happen. It was a heavy price. The woman's life was cut short and, even worse, their first child would belong to the Jackal. Later, when Melchior had second thoughts about what he had done, he broke the contract. While the woman was pregnant with their child, he smuggled both mother and son away, hoping to hide them from the Jackal's notice."

Jack continued in a somber voice. "But no matter how far he went, he couldn't run from the Corruption. As the Jackal's poison set in, Melchior's love for the mortal woman became increasingly selfish. He grew jealous and possessive, fearing that someone might take her away from him. And the more he lived with these twisted, prickly thoughts, the more he started to resemble them. His once beautiful appearance was changed into something small, dark, and monstrous. He became a shriveled man who looked more porcupine than human."

Edward's face grew pale. *Wait a minute. Did he just say the woman's life was cut short?* The same thing had happened to Edward's mother. Not only that, but he remembered Artemis and Sariel referring to Mr. Spines as "Melchior" when they were on the train. He didn't like where this line of thinking was going. The implications of what that would mean were horrible. He bit his lip anxiously. *It can't be*, he reassured himself. *It's only a coincidence.*

"Melchior and his wife began fighting daily, and all of the happiness he had known on Earth began to melt away. It was after a particularly vicious argument that Melchior decided to abandon his wife and newborn son. The small part of him that was still a Guardian realized that it would be better for him to leave them than to allow the Corruption to fully take hold. He hoped that she would be happier without him, and that maybe the Jackal would leave her alone if he were gone.

The woman died thirteen years later without their son ever meeting his father. The doctors never did identify the disease that killed her, but Melchior knew the truth. It was because of the contract he'd signed with the Jackal that she died in the prime of her life."

Edward squirmed uncomfortably. He couldn't look at Jack, couldn't bear to hear the rest of the story. But he also couldn't bring himself to leave the room. He just sat there, feeling stunned, with his palms sweating and his heart hammering in his chest.

Jack shook his head sadly. "After his mother's death, the state arranged for Melchior's son to be sent to a boarding school called the Foundry. But it was under surveillance by some of the Jackal's low-ranking forces. After a year at that miserable school, the boy developed a terrible itch between his shoulders. Soon after that, he sprouted wings. That's when Melchior came back into the story. He rescued his son before a Groundling nicknamed Whiplash Scruggs could capture him and sever his newly sprouted wings, a sure death for any Guardian. The boy escaped and then used one of Melchior's inventions to transport himself here."

No, it can't be true! Spines can't be my, my . . . Edward felt dizzy. Bridgette looked at him with a concerned expression. He was trembling all over, unwilling to believe the story he'd just heard.

It's over. A cruel voice kept repeating itself over and over in his head. *You thought you had a fresh start, didn't you? Thought that everything would be different up here. But you were wrong. You're the son of a Groundling. And you'll end up just like him, wait and see. Having wings doesn't make you a Guardian. You're destined to fail, just like he did. He killed your mother and would have given you to the Jackal.*

Edward felt like he was going to be sick. The room was suddenly stuffy and the air too thick to breathe. Tabitha said, "Whiplash Scruggs? I know that name! 'Scruggs' is Moloc, one of our fiercest enemies!"

Jack gave the young Guardian a worried

glance. "We all know Moloc by reputation. But when I found out about his contact with the boy, the question I had was *why* did the Jackal assign one of his most fearsome commanders to pursue someone who didn't even know that he was a Guardian? Even if he was Melchior's son."

Jack reached over to one of the books on his shelf and removed a volume with green silk binding. "And I believe this is the answer. It's an excerpt from *Bridges Between the Worlds*, a clever bit of prophecy disguised as a children's rhyme."

Jack cleared his throat and after lowering a pair of half spectacles, read,

*"There are seven bridges between the worlds
and five of them are broken,
the sixth one has no rails to hold,
and the seventh one was stolen.
Captive then, the wand'ring dead,
for an epoch the world's turn.
When halfway from the mortal realm,
a builder will return.*

His twisted tongue will utter song,
the champion will arise,
but fallen Groundling or gentle Guard,
his choices will decide."

There was silence as Jack closed the book. Edward had barely had enough time to process what Jack had said about Mr. Spines being his father, and now he was being asked to believe that he, Edward, was some kind of hero? It couldn't be possible, could it? Edward stared at Jack, his mind spinning. He wanted to run away, to get to some quiet place and build card houses. His hand strayed to his pocket where the deck was hidden, seeking reassurance. He found the box and gripped it hard, trying to keep his hands from shaking.

The faun continued, "Ever since the Jackal fell, tearing apart the seven bridges that led to the Higher Places, we mortals have been trapped here in the Woodbine. This world, which was once just a stopping place for newly arrived souls, has become a prison that keeps us from moving forward. The rhyme speaks of the champion that will repair the Jackal's destruction and set us all free so that we can travel back up the Seven Bridges to the Higher Places. The souls trapped in the Woodbine have waited centuries for this person to come. And after much discussion, Tollers and I believe that the person mentioned in this rhyme is with us now."

The faun turned to look at the tall, skinny boy with black wings. "Edward, will you come forward?"

Edward stood, looking gangly and uncertain in the firelight. Every eye in the room was staring at him and he felt the color rise in his cheeks.

Jack smiled broadly and gave him an encouraging pat on the arm.

"Tollers and I believe that this, my friends, is the Bridge Builder mentioned in the prophecy. As the rhyme states, he's 'halfway from the mortal realm,' which can only refer to the son of a Guardian and a mortal. Tabitha and Jemial, meet Edward Macleod, the one that the Jackal asked for in the contract signed by Melchior. We believe that he is the champion that will one day rebuild the Seven Bridges. The Jackal must have known it would be Melchior's son, so he tried to destroy him in infancy."

Jemial and Tabitha looked at Edward skeptically. Edward could tell right away that he didn't fit their ideas of what a heroic character should look like.

Jemial cleared his throat. "Jack, your authority on these matters is well-known," he said awkwardly. "But, with all due respect, I seriously doubt that the text was referring to this boy. I'm sure it must be a coincidence." The big Guardian glanced at Edward and said, "That bit of rhyme has been around for a long time. I don't think it was ever meant to be taken literally."

"And if it *was* true, it couldn't have been referring to the son of a fallen Guardian," Tabitha said, eyeing Edward coolly. "If there really is a Bridge Builder, he would be greater than Mi'kael[1] himself. Nobody has ever been able to sing a Song powerful enough to rebuild the Seven Bridges!" She arched an eyebrow at

1 Mi'kael has been universally recognized as the most powerful commander of the Guardian Forces.

Edward. "And I really think that the Bridge Builder wouldn't have a problem with speech, either." She crossed her arms. "There's no way this *boy* could possibly be him."

"Oh, but that's where you're mistaken," Jack said, his eyes twinkling. "The rhyme also mentions a 'twisted tongue.' I think it suggests further evidence in Edward's favor."

Edward stared at the floor. He'd never asked for this, to be considered some great, prophetic hero. All he wanted to do was rescue his mom. But, on the other hand, what if everything Jack was saying was true? A glimmer of hope flared in his chest. What if the prophecy really meant that he was destined to be different than his father? That he actually *was* destined to be a hero? Could it be possible?

Resentment over Tabitha and Jemial's outright dismissal of his potential seethed inside him. They didn't even know him. Maybe he was untrained, but it didn't mean that he couldn't learn.

Suddenly, an all too familiar voice sounded from the doorway.

"You, young apprentice, are wrong. The boy *is* the Bridge Builder," the voice said.

No one had heard the front door swing open, or the silent footsteps that had crept into the room. But all eyes were now turned on the small, crumpled-looking figure that stood at the edge of the common room. The stumpy man had spiny hair that pointed in all directions from underneath a stovepipe hat. His breath came in ragged gasps, and his glittering eyes swept the room in a glare of defiance.

"He *is* the one. I've known it all along. After all, I should. I'm his father."

+ Chapter Four +

SPINES

Edward Macleod stared at the creature that had once been Melchior, feeling his stomach twist in desperation. It was impossible to believe that this *thing*, this *creature* that had recklessly promised him to the Jackal before he was born was actually his *father*.

Edward stepped back as Mr. Spines hobbled toward him.

"I wanted to tell you everything," Spines rasped. "But your mother needs help, and I didn't know if you would agree to go with me if I told you the truth. You must learn to use your wings, Edward, and discover how to use your other powers so that we can reach her. I can train you."

"Don't t-talk to me about m-my mother!" Edward fired back. "Y-you have no r-right. It was b-because of you she d-died. Y-you would have given me to the Jackal!" he shouted.

Edward stood there, glaring at Mr. Spines and shaking with rage. He'd never felt so angry in his entire life.

There was a ring of steel as Jemial unsheathed his curved sword. After leveling it at Mr. Spines's neck he said, "Melchior, you know that if a Guardian falls, they're no longer welcome in the Woodbine." The huge man towered over the prickly creature. "You are in violation of the law."

Everyone in the room held their breath. Mr. Spines didn't flinch. He gazed directly into Jemial's eyes and said in a low voice, "I don't serve the Jackal, I broke my contract. I've come to protect the boy and help him find his mother and then I'll leave for good. Would a Groundling do that?"

Tabitha spoke, looking angry. "How do we know he's not lying?" she shouted. "It could be a trick! The Jackal could be luring us to his Lair so that he can destroy us!" She glared at Melchior. "He's says he's not a Groundling but just look at him. The Corruption is too great. There can't be any part of a Guardian left in that hideous mess."

"She brings up a good point," Jemial said slowly. "Groundlings are known for deception and he could be lying," The big Guardian turned to look at Tabitha. "However, it is also the policy of Guardians not to judge books by their covers, young apprentice."

Tabitha stared at Jemial with openmouthed surprise. She looked ready to retaliate, but, with evident struggle, held her tongue.

Jemial turned back to Melchior, the Guardian's sword still positioned at his throat. Then, after an excruciatingly long moment, Jemial lowered his weapon.

"By the Beggar Lord," he said softly, "I would love nothing better than to see you gone forever. However, it isn't my decision to make. I'll leave it to the Council to decide what should be done." He sheathed his sword and turned to Jack. "I'd like for you to keep him here for a little while, if you don't mind. As soon as I get to Estrella, I'll notify the Council and they'll arrange an escort. By Woodbine law, he must stand trial. It's the only way to get to the bottom of all this."

Mr. Spines gave the Guardian a stony look. Jemial motioned for Tabitha to follow him.

"Come, apprentice. We have work elsewhere."

"But he's a traitor! We don't need the Council on this! We should just eliminate him like we would any other Groundling," Tabitha said angrily.

"It is not your decision," Jemial said firmly.

"But . . ."

"Abide by the law, apprentice," Jemial said evenly.

Tabitha's mouth worked soundlessly. Shaking with rage, she stomped from the room. Jemial stayed just long enough to incline his head courteously to Jack and Joyce before following after his angry apprentice.

Edward wished he could leave, too, to get as far away from Mr. Spines as he could. Growing up, he'd often wondered what had happened to his father. And when things were really bad at his boarding school, he'd dreamed that his father would come back one day, a heroic figure that would take him away from that terrible situation.

Edward glanced at Melchior and frowned. His father had saved him, but he was no hero. And now that he had come back, Edward wanted nothing to do with him. He couldn't get over the part of the story where Melchior had agreed to give him to the Jackal to get what he wanted. Even if Melchior hadn't actually gone through with it, what kind of a person would agree to such a thing? It was unthinkable!

Edward was mulling over these dark thoughts when suddenly there was a noise at the cottage entrance. The door banged open and, to everyone's surprise, Tabitha, her pearly wings fluttering with agitation, rushed back into the cottage followed by her master.

"It's Whiplash Scruggs and a troop of Groundlings! They must have followed Melchior here," Tabitha shouted.

Jemial flashed Melchior an expression filled with doubt. His voice took on a dangerous tone. "Either that, or someone has led him directly to us."

✦ Chapter Five ✦

ESCAPE!

Through an open window, Edward could hear the faint barks of Whiplash Scruggs's hounds in the distance. Edward still saw Scruggs and his deadly pair of silver scissors every time he closed his eyes. He was terrified of the cruel teacher, but at least now he had friends to help protect him. He wasn't going to give up without a fight.

"I am not working with Scruggs!" Mr. Spines wheezed. His face looked haggard and pale. "The Jackal has spies posted everywhere, keeping watch on every new arrival in the Woodbine. I did my best to cover my tracks, but as you can plainly see . . ." Mr. Spines indicated his own withered and crumpled form. "The Corruption has made it difficult for me to even move. If I don't have some medical attention soon, I probably won't survive much longer."

Spines seemed much smaller and uglier than when Edward first met him on the train. The creature had more spines growing out from beneath his stovepipe hat than ever, and his jacket was riddled with holes where new spikes were starting to poke through. He was starting to look more like a monster than a man.

Mr. Spines coughed and continued, "Whiplash Scruggs doesn't care about any of you. All he wants is the boy." Melchior indicated Edward with a sharp nod.

"W-well, h-he can't have me!" Edward shot back. He was starting to panic.

"Of course he can't," Spines said, shooting Edward a withered look. "Trust me, boy, with whatever I have left, I will fight to keep you safe from him. But we must hurry if we're to escape his notice." He turned his bloodshot eyes on Jack. "Is there a back door?" Melchior ran his tongue across his yellowed teeth.

Jack nodded. "Yes, Joyce had me install a passage for just such an emergency. I'll take you to it."

"You're going to help him? After what he's

done?" Tabitha asked, looking amazed.

Jack nodded at the young Guardian. "I believe that Melchior is telling us the truth. I'll do all I can to help. If he says he's against the Jackal and wants to help Edward, then that's good enough for me."

"That's the stupidest idea I've ever heard!" Tabitha shouted. "He could betray us all!"

"It's true," Jemial said. "With all due respect, Jack, do you realize what you're risking? If he's lying, there could be terrible consequences." Jemial glanced at Edward. "How do we know Melchior's not going to turn Edward over to the Jackal? You know how the Groundlings are, they'll do anything to get into their master's good graces." Jemial shook his head, worried. "I think delivering him to the Council is the safest bet."

In the brief silence that followed, Edward could hear the barking of Whiplash Scruggs's hounds growing closer. They needed to hurry.

To Edward's surprise, the faun didn't appear in the least bit concerned by the Guardians' doubt. He tapped his pipe out in his palm thoughtfully and said, "Thank you both for your counsel, but I haven't changed my mind." Jack glanced at Melchior and smiled. "I believe everyone deserves a second chance."

Jemial sighed. "You leave me no choice, Jack. I'll have to report this," he said. "But for friendship's sake, I'll wait to do it until tomorrow morning. Melchior's presence in the Woodbine will not be received well by the Council. You might think he's still a Guardian but most of my colleagues won't. They'll probably want to see him hunted down and destroyed as soon as possible."

Edward thought Tabitha looked ready to explode with anger as she watched the exchange. But one look from Jemial and she bottled what was sure to be an angry retort.

A howl interrupted Edward's thoughts, sending a chill down his spine. Scruggs was nearly at the door!

"Is the house protected?" Jemial demanded.

"We had a couple of Guardians do a Shield Song several years back, but it probably needs to be sung again," Jack said.

"I'll sing the Song of Warding. It should reinforce the shield on the cottage and hold Scruggs off for a while." The big Guardian turned to Tabitha and said firmly, "I want you to go with them. Help the boy find his mother."

Tabitha looked aghast. "But she was captured by the Jackal! No Guardians can penetrate his Lair. And besides, you promised that we would go to the graduation ceremony. I've waited so long!"

"Tabitha, this is not open to discussion. You're to protect the boy. We can address your graduation later," Jemial commanded.

"But . . ." Tabitha complained.

"That's an order, young one."

Tabitha looked livid. "You're making a huge mis—"

But she didn't finish her sentence. Jemial towered over her, his magnificent silver wings stretched out to their full width. The apprentice's eyes grew wide as she stared at her master. The older Guardian's wings glowed with magical radiance, throwing the room into sharp, shadowy contrast. Everyone, including Edward, shielded his or her eyes. Jemial looked furious, and the look on Tabitha's face said she knew she had gone too far.

"YOU ARE MY APPRENTICE AND YOU WILL OBEY!" Jemial thundered. Sparks shot from his fingertips and his curved sword glowed with an unearthly radiance. Tabitha stared up at Jemial, and although Edward could tell she was afraid, she was trying hard not to show it.

Suddenly, a loud *B-B-BOOM!* rattled the interior of the cottage. Edward looked around wildly. *What was that?*

"It's Scruggs! He's attacking the shield on the cottage. Everyone please go down the hall to my study. The entrance to the secret passage is there. Quickly!" Jack said, motioning to Edward, Melchior, and Tabitha.

Jemial withdrew a small flute from his pocket and began to play the Song of Warding. Beautiful music filled the air and a faint, golden glow materialized around the outside of the cottage. As the song took effect, Whiplash Scruggs's attacks seemed to grow more muffled.

Melchior and Tabitha hurried down the hall.

But before Jack could follow, Bridgette pulled him aside. Edward paused in the doorway, wanting the chance to say good-bye to Bridgette before he left. He couldn't help but overhear what she said to her uncle.

"I'm going with them, Uncle," she whispered.

"No, it's too dangerous, Bridgette. Moloc is one of the most vile creatures in the Jackal's army. You could be seriously hurt!" Jack answered.

Bridgette looked resolute. "I'm sorry. I know you're trying to protect me, but I *need* to go." She glanced at Edward and then quickly turned back to her uncle. "Remember what we talked about? I believe that *this* is the reason I'm here, the reason I didn't go immediately to the Higher Places like my sister."

After a long moment, Jack nodded, but he didn't look happy. "So be it. Come with me."

The faun trotted quickly out of the living room, leading Bridgette and Edward down a narrow hallway. Edward knew it was selfish and would put Bridgette in danger, but he was glad she was coming with him.

BOOOOOM! The sound came again, this time from the opposite side of the house. Edward, who was waiting in the back room, glanced outside a nearby window and saw curling wisps of yellow smoke rising from the lawn.

Edward tried not to panic, and silently prayed that somehow Jemial's song would still work.

Just buy us a few minutes more so that we can escape!

Then the booming sound came again. And this time, to everyone's horror, the sound was accompanied by a loud *CRACK!*

Scruggs had broken through!

Jack rushed to a large wardrobe in the corner of his study and opened the doors to reveal a hidden passage.

"Quick, through here!" the faun commanded. "Follow this passage all the way to the dock at the end. I'll send a signal to the boatman; he's a friend of mine and will help you. Good-bye and good luck!"

Bridgette caught her uncle in a fierce hug and Edward could see tears in both of their eyes. Then the faun pushed the wardrobe doors closed and the passageway was suddenly plunged into total darkness.

Edward heard a sharp scratching noise. Then a flicker suddenly illuminated Mr. Spines's ugly face. He was holding a light encased in a tiny, silver box covered with gears.

"Follow me!" He growled and hobbled down the damp passageway. Edward and the others followed the tiny, glimmering light as it bobbed off into the distance.

Debris rained down, and several muffled explosions echoed above them. After what seemed like an eternity, they finally reached the end. Spines climbed up a small ladder and shoved hard against a thick, wooden trapdoor.

To everyone's surprise, they emerged inside a hollow tree trunk. They climbed out through a huge gap in the massive tree right next to the riverbank. A rickety dock was about thirty yards away to the north, sprawling over a rapidly flowing river. Spines, Tabitha, and Bridgette raced toward it.

Edward didn't follow immediately. He could hear the sounds of a battle coming from behind him and was worried. He climbed up on a low tree branch and looked back at Jack's house. Underneath the cloudy sky, flames were beginning to lick the sides of the thatched cottage. He hoped everyone else would be all right. Edward jumped down, and sprinted to catch up with the others. Nobody frightened him more than Whiplash Scruggs. The thought that he was near made Edward feel sick to his stomach.

"Scruggs will find out we're gone soon," Mr. Spines yelled back at him. "Hurry."

As they struggled down the shoreline, the sound of baying hounds filled the air, followed by a flurry of deep-throated barks.

Spines stared in the direction of the cottage and let out a long, low hiss.

"He already knows!" And in spite of his severely weakened condition, the stunted creature shot off down the dock.

"I'm coming!" a voice floated across the river toward them. Edward could make out a figure clad in heavy boots and a leather jerkin standing on a large boat that reminded him a little bit of a sturdy gondola. A stocky man was holding a long pole and was pushing the boat toward them as quickly as he could. With relief, Edward realized that this must be the boatman that Jack had mentioned!

An eerie howl split the air, much closer than before. The skin on the back of Edward's neck prickled. Whiplash Scruggs and his Groundlings were not far behind!

"Help!" Tabitha shouted, her wings fluttering in agitation.

"I got Jack's signal. Is there trouble?" the boatman shouted back as he poled the boat into position.

"We're being pursued by Groundlings," Mr. Spines growled.

The stocky man nodded quickly. "Hop aboard then, but be careful not to touch the water. You're on the banks of the Lethye. Can't afford to have anyone lose their marbles."

Edward had no idea what the boatman meant, but he was careful to stay dry as he climbed in. Then he glanced behind him and immediately wished he hadn't. Whiplash Scruggs was almost to the river.

"Go! Go! GO!" Edward shouted. "He's here!"

WHOOOSH! Something hot whistled past Edward's head, narrowly missing his ear. Edward raised his hand to his cheek, feeling a slight burning sensation. Fortunately, the flaming object had only singed him.

"It's an Oroborus!" Tabitha shouted. Edward turned and spotted the blazing ring as it soared over a nearby thicket of pine trees. If it had flown any closer, it would have taken his head off!

Tabitha quickly undid a clasp at her blue sash and withdrew her golden ring. "Everybody stay as far down on the deck as you can! I'll guard us from the air!"

She gazed down at her ring and shouted, "*QADOS!*" Instantly, the golden hoop was encircled in a flickering ring of blue flames. Then, with a mighty downward flap of her wings, Tabitha launched herself into the air.

Above the pine trees in the distance, the Oroborus had completed its arc and was now returning to its owner, streaking toward them like a flaming comet.

Whiplash Scruggs stood waiting for it on the

dock. His troops of low-ranking Groundlings spread out behind him in various states of decay. They were terrifying. The only Groundlings that Edward had encountered so far had looked human, except for their unnaturally pale blue eyes and sharp teeth. But apparently those human trappings were reserved for the highest ranked soldiers in the Jackal's army, a "costume" of sorts that hid their true, corrupted bodies. This throng of gibbering creatures on the bank was exposed for what they really were.

Edward cringed. Could such things have ever been beautiful Guardians? Many were half-rotten, covered with leprous sores. A few others had a misshapen wing or a crumpled bunch of feathers sticking out of their twisted backs. Their ugly faces had fangs, snouts, or vulture-like beaks, and every one of them had eyes of the palest blue.

As Tabitha swooped through the air, the Groundlings were distracted from the boat where Edward, Bridgette, and Spines were hiding. Instead they focused on the young Guardian. They jeered as Tabitha dove and swooped, trying to avoid the deadly weapon that seemed to track her every movement.

She's not going to be able to dodge it forever, Edward thought grimly. *One wrong move and she's done for!*

Even though no one had explained how the weapon worked, Edward quickly figured it out. The Oroborus had been designed to seek out Guardians and was guided to the closest enemy target with deadly accuracy. Because Tabitha was nearest, the ring was after her. He assumed Guardian rings worked the same way, seeking their opposite in battle and honing in on evil like a magnet.

Edward could only stare, mouth agape, as he watched the Guardian fly. He'd never gotten to see anyone fly before. He watched her every move as she darted majestically through the air. He'd never seen such an amazing sight.

He really wanted to know what it was like to have such power. His wings were built for flying, but he needed to learn how to use them first. Perhaps what Mr. Spines and Bridgette had said was true. He needed to be trained. But it seemed impossible that he could ever come close to the mastery that Tabitha possessed.

And Tabitha wasn't just flying. She was fighting, too. When the Oroborus got too close, Tabitha used her own ring as a shield. Edward watched flashes of red fire collide with blue sparks as she successfully deflected each of the weapon's successive attacks with her slim, golden circle.

Edward had nearly forgotten about Whiplash Scruggs while watching Tabitha's performance. But he was brought back to the present when he heard the fearsome commander bellow an order to his soldiers.

Up in the sky, Tabitha continued her acrobatic dance, narrowly avoiding the Oroborus. Edward could tell that she was getting tired. She wasn't making as many fancy loops and dives anymore. It seemed to take all of her strength just to deflect the relentless ring.

Suddenly, all of the Groundlings gave a shout, saying the same, guttural word in unison.

"NSH!"

Circles of red flame appeared around the

Oroboruses that each of the Groundlings held in their fists. Edward had mistakenly thought that Whiplash Scruggs had possessed the only one! With a shout, the other Groundlings threw their Oroboruses into the air, hurling them toward the sole defender that hovered above Edward's boat.

Edward's mind raced. If he didn't do something fast, Tabitha would be cut to ribbons!

Suddenly, like it had once before, a strange word popped into his mind. It was the same word that he'd used before to repel an attack from Lilith and Henry Asmoday, two of the Jackal's most powerful servants when he was in Los Angeles. He could feel a tingling sensation building inside of him as he turned his head skyward, determining an angle where the swiftly moving evil rings could be intercepted. Then, after steadying himself for the tremendous burst of energy that was sure to come, he stood up on the deck. Extending his fingers in the direction of the flaming weapons he shouted,

"*HISTALEK!*"

There was a flash of blue light and the

burning smell of ozone. Lightning arced from Edward's extended fingertips, snaking skyward to intercept the dozen hoops of red fire.

KERRACCCKKKK! The electric shock from Edward's fingertips hit the evil rings with an explosion of sparks.

Broken pieces of Oroborus showered down all around the boat, peppering the water with little splashes. Edward swayed on his feet. It felt as if all his strength had drained from his body.

His eyes lost focus as the world spun crazily around him.

He heard a muffled shout from Bridgette as his legs folded beneath him and his long body crashed down toward the bottom of the boat, landing with a *THUNK!* He didn't see his precious deck of cards tumble from his pocket and fall into the water as he hit the hard, wooden deck.

Everything went black.

Chapter Six

A VEILED THREAT

A shout of rage echoed from the shoreline as Whiplash Scruggs watched the boatman pole the vessel into swifter waters. Edward's soggy kings and queens, deuces and jacks drifted downstream in the rushing current.

Scruggs barked a command to his troops. Seconds later, the air was filled with flaming arrows, arcing high through the air and descending toward the ship. The arrows splashed into the water all around the little boat, hissing and filling the air with smoke. But whether it was luck, or just bad shooting by the enemy, the Groundlings missed their target.

Under the expert guidance of Al the boatman, the vessel swept down the rushing current and was soon out of range, lost to view around a bend in the river.

Back at the dock, Scruggs reached into the pocket of his white coat and removed a cheroot cigar. As the smoke curled up around his ears, his eyes narrowed beneath his bushy, black brows. He noticed something that had washed up on the shore and, bending down, he picked it up with his chubby fingers.

It was an ace of spades with a grinning skull in its center. Scruggs crumpled the card in his meaty fist. It had happened again. The boy had evaded him three times!

While Scruggs contemplated this unfortunate turn of events, two other Groundlings walked up to him. Both of them appeared human, although they were anything but. They had been watching all that happened on the bank and were eager to gloat over Scruggs's lack of success.

Whiplash himself was disguised as a heavyset man wearing an enormous white suit and he towered over the thin, elderly looking Groundlings next to him. In another setting, one might have even mistaken them for kindly grandparents. But Henry and Lilith Asmoday were both ancient and terrible, and, although their bodies looked human, their souls were long gone.

Henry wore a straw boater and resembled a mortal man in his seventies. He stood with his arm linked with Lilith, an aging woman carrying a silk parasol. Although it was 1921 on Earth, their clothing would have seemed old-fashioned by most people's standards.

Lilith's eyes were covered by dark glasses. They hid the injury that Edward had given her at their last meeting. She hadn't been wounded in a fight with a Guardian for over three thousand years and was looking forward to making Edward pay!

Henry had his hands in his pockets as he surveyed the spot where the boat had been just moments before. Squinting after it, he said, "Well, gee Moloc, that didn't go according to plan, did it? Chances are, the master ain't going to be pleased. Nope. Not one bit, I reckon."

As he finished his statement, Henry flashed a sharp-toothed grin at Scruggs, enjoying his obvious discomfort.

"Mr. Scruggs, why don't you just scurry back on home and tell the Jackal that you're not ready for this assignment? I'm sure he'll find something else for you to do. Henry and I can handle things here just fine on our own," Lilith purred at him.

Scruggs paled. He'd already failed his master twice. He knew what returning empty-handed meant. The last thing he needed was Henry and Lilith running back to the master with news of his failure. He dropped his cigar on the dewy grass and grounded it out with his heel.

"Rest assured, my friends, I have no intention of returning at this rather inopportune time," Scruggs drawled. "This is merely an unfortunate setback, not a *failed* attempt. I *will* find the boy."

Henry chuckled and set his straw boater back on his head. After brushing at his gray, handlebar moustache with his finger, he replied, "Well, you'd better find him soon, son." Henry's pale blue eyes twinkled with malice. "See, the Jackal told us to keep an eye on you. Said that if you couldn't catch the boy, he'd turn it over to Lil and I to take care of the situation."

He eyed Scruggs flabby form and grinned hungrily, exposing rows of pointed teeth.

"And we'd just love to have you for dinner."

Chapter Seven

HEALING

"But it was one of the Ten Words of Power!"
Tabitha said. Her voice was an urgent whisper.
"Even when you were a Guardian, you couldn't
have taught him that. Those words are reserved for
high-ranking officers. Where did he learn it?"

Mr. Spines replied huskily, "I don't know.
But since the boy is destined to become an
officer someday, perhaps the greatest there ever
was, there could be many mysteries about him."
The spiny man's eyes narrowed with concern.
"But he's not ready to use such power yet. It
could destroy him before he even learns how to
fly. He must have training."

Mr. Spines and Tabitha were in a back
bedroom of the boatman's shack. Spines was
slumped in a hardback chair, almost too weak to
move. Edward was lying unconscious on a cot with

a kerosene lamp positioned on a nearby table.

Tabitha looked down at Edward with concern. It had been hours since the attack and Edward didn't seem to be improving. His face looked even paler than usual and his breathing was shallow.

"He needs healing. A Song of Restoration should do it," Mr. Spines suggested quietly.

"You'd like that, wouldn't you?" Tabitha replied sharply. "If I sang it, you'd get the benefits, too."

There was a pause. Then Mr. Spines admitted, "It wouldn't be the same as a full chorus of Guardians singing it, but it would help. But right now, I'm only thinking of the boy. Using that word has weakened him severely. Remember, he's half mortal. He could go into shock. And we don't have time to let him heal on his own. That could take days."

There was a long pause as Tabitha considered Mr. Spines's words. Finally, after a long moment, she spoke. "My flute fell out of my pocket during the battle at the river. The song won't do very much without an instrument."

Mr. Spines paused a moment and then replied, "In my pocket you'll find a wooden sphere. Open it."

Tabitha did as she was told, grimacing a little as she reached into the withered man's grimy little pocket. She removed the smooth, round ball and looked at it closely.

"I don't see a latch."

Mr. Spines coughed. "Come now, I'd expect a little more out of an apprentice. Sing the *word*, girl."

Tabitha looked annoyed. She clearly didn't like being lectured by a fallen Guardian. She looked at the smooth, wooden sphere and softly sang the Guardian word for open.

"*Sisma.*"

A crack of white light appeared around the perimeter of the globe. Then it split in two, revealing a small, glowing pebble in its center.

"Hand it to me," Spines said quietly.

Tabitha didn't argue. She placed the glowing speck in Mr. Spines's extended hand. The porcupine man stared at it for a moment then raised it to his leathery lips and breathed on it.

The speck glowed brightly for a moment and then began to grow, gradually twisting and shaping itself into a small, elegantly crafted harp. It was of such exquisite beauty and craftsmanship that Tabitha couldn't help but be impressed.

"You made this?" she asked as Mr. Spines handed her the delicate instrument. He nodded.

"Yes, it was one of the last things I made before I fell. Because the Jackal doesn't allow his servants to sing Songs of Power, I've had to keep it hidden."

Tabitha stroked the strings experimentally. A beautiful harmony of sound filled the tiny room. She raised an eyebrow appreciatively. Then she closed her eyes and, after spending a moment plucking out the melody, she began to sing the Song of Restoration.

The dim light in the boatman's shack grew brighter. The walls, which had been a weather-beaten gray, suddenly shone as if recently cleaned. Dust and cobwebs dissolved, and the musty shack was filled with the delicious scent of roses.

But most important were the changes

happening to Edward and Mr. Spines. The Song's effect was the most pronounced on Edward, whose pale face began to glow with health and whose breathing grew regular. Seconds later his eyes fluttered open, just in time to see the effect that the Song of Restoration was having on Mr. Spines.

The extra quills that had sprouted as a result of his most recent disobedience to the Jackal seemed to melt back into his body. His face, which had been a chalky white color, regained a more normal hue. His tiny hands, which had been bent and twisted, began to straighten. And although the Song could do little to restore him to the Guardian he once was, Edward caught the briefest glimpse of something in his father's face that he'd never seen before. He saw the shadow of Melchior, and in that moment, he saw someone who looked very much like himself.

But the illusion faded the instant Tabitha stopped singing, and Mr. Spines looked just as he had when Edward met him for the first time on the train.

Tabitha was out of breath after singing such

a powerful song. She glanced down at Edward as she lowered the harp. "Feeling better?" she asked, not too unkindly.

Edward nodded. "Th-thanks. That w-was pretty am-amuh-amazing."

Tabitha didn't respond right away, but sniffed imperiously and handed the harp back to Melchior. As she stood up she mentioned, "It was nothing special. It's a Guardian's duty to help others in need. Besides," she looked at him meaningfully, "I don't know how you did it, but you saved my feathers back there. Thank you."

Tabitha quickly turned and walked out of the tiny room, leaving Edward alone with his father.

There was an awkward pause. Edward sat up slowly and stared out the window, trying not to make eye contact with Mr. Spines. His father removed a gold pocket watch and glanced at the time. Neither of them seemed to know what to say.

Edward finally broke the uncomfortable silence. "W-where're Artemis and S-Sariel?" he asked in a flat voice. It was the only thing he could think to ask. He'd met Mr. Spines's apprentices before and didn't really care to see them again. Because of the Jackal's Corruption, they'd been transformed from Guardians into a white ermine and flying toad. His main recollection of the two creatures was that they bickered constantly. At least they weren't here, adding to his frustration.

"Hiding at my old workshop here in the Woodbine," Spines replied. "I told them to stay there until I sent for them."

Edward continued staring out the window, at a total loss as to what else to say. He knew he needed to work with Mr. Spines to rescue his mother, but he was still very angry at his father, and he wasn't ready to start making nice.

I just want to find my mom. That's all. Then hopefully he'll leave us alone.

Edward was relieved when Bridgette opened the door with a concerned expression on her face, interrupting the awkward moment. She looked over at Edward and then at Mr. Spines and blushed.

"Oh, I'm sorry. I just heard that you were okay, and I . . . I didn't mean to interrupt. I'll

just wait outside," she said, backing out of
the room.

"N-nuh-no! Yuh-you're not interrupting
anything." Edward leapt up from the cot and
followed Bridgette out of the room.

Spines noticed Edward's eagerness to get
away. He sighed, running his hand through
his head of spiny prickles. His weathered face
looked incredibly ancient and his eyes glistened
with unshed tears. And as the fallen Guardian
gazed after his retreating son, his leathery lips
whispered the phrase he'd rehearsed and had
tried so often to say.

"I love you son."

Chapter Eight ✦

THE BOATMAN'S SHACK

"After you passed out, Tabitha sang a Song
of Motivation that helped us pick up speed.
We traveled all afternoon to get here, to the
boatman's house," Bridgette said, filling Edward
in on everything he had missed.

As Bridgette ushered Edward into the main
living area of the tiny shack, she glanced up at him
shyly. "By the way, that was pretty amazing what
you did back there, destroying the Oroboruses
before they hit Tabitha. While you were
unconscious, Tabitha kept going on and on about
it. She didn't know how you'd done it."

Edward was thrilled by Bridgette's compliment.

"Oh, w-well I duh-d-don't r-really know how
I did it either," Edward stuttered. "I was j-just
lucky it wuh-worked."

His hand reached automatically for his deck

of cards he kept in his pocket, seeking the reassuring comfort of the pack. He always did that when he was nervous.

With a start, he realized they weren't there.

"What h-happened to my c-cards?" he asked, looking alarmed.

Bridgette winced. "I'm sorry, Edward. They fell into the river when you were unconscious," she said.

The blood drained from Edward's face. He'd had the same deck since he was three years old. The day that his mother bought them for him was one of his favorite memories. He had built an elaborate card house right on the floor of an unusual toyshop in Portland. Edward's mother had been so delighted that she bought him the deck on the spot. Just having the deck with him made him feel more confident, safer.

Edward looked around, trying to shake his grief over the loss of his cards. He didn't want Bridgette to know he was upset about losing them. It would probably seem like a silly thing to be sad about to her.

He cleared his throat, and tried to look

like the loss of his cards didn't bother him. "Whatever," he said casually, shoving his hands in his pockets. "They were just cards."

He focused his attention on his new surroundings, trying his best to look unconcerned. Bridgette stared up at him with a sympathetic expression. In spite of Edward's best efforts, she could tell the loss had affected him deeply.

The rickety house reminded Edward of pictures he'd seen of the fishermen's houses in Cape Cod. Nets and floats were the primary wall decorations, offset by various items that had been found washed up on the banks of the river. Tabitha's Song of Restoration had had quite an effect on this room, too. Everything was clean and shining in the firelight.

The boatman was sitting on a comfortable sofa with a steaming mug of hot chocolate in his meaty hand. Tabitha had taken a seat on an old barrel next to him, with her pearly wings folded primly behind her. Bridgette ushered Edward forward and formally introduced him to the boatman.

"Edward, this is Al," Bridgette said.

Edward mumbled, "H-hello," and shook the man's outstretched hand. He winced, hating the fact that every time he opened his mouth the words just didn't come out right.

"Thank you for rescuing us. If you hadn't come along when you did, I don't think we would have made it," Bridgette chimed in.

"Not a problem," he said cheerfully. "Usually I'm just boating the new arrivals to the Woodbine back and forth to the docks, up and down the river, so a little extra excitement was welcome."

The boatman glanced over at a small wood-burning stove in the corner of the living room and wiped a calloused hand across his forehead.

"Is it too hot in here?" he asked. "I could douse the fire a little if you guys are too uncomfortable."

"I'm f-fine," Edward said, trying to be polite. The others in the room agreed. Apparently, the boatman was not used to heating his house for company, because the stocky man kept pulling at his heavy shirt, trying to keep it from sticking to his sweaty belly.

Edward heard footsteps behind him and noticed that Mr. Spines had joined them, taking a seat slightly behind the rest of the group.

Ugh, Edward thought. He stood up from his chair and walked over to the living room window.

The clouds had cleared away. In the star-studded sky, a huge, silver moon shone down on the river, reflecting off its surface. He couldn't help wondering if they really had escaped Whiplash Scruggs, or if he was still somewhere nearby, tracking them down while he'd been unconscious. He was sure that Scruggs had only been temporarily put off. His insides quivered, dreading another encounter with the horrible Groundling. His fingers twitched, automatically reaching for his pocket, but there was nothing there. No reassuring feeling of the deck he'd always carried.

"Don't worry," Al said, watching Edward with concern. "I made sure to cover all of our tracks from the boat to the house with water from the Lethye."

Edward glanced at Al, looking confused. What good would river water do to hide them from Whiplash Scruggs? Wouldn't the evil Groundling be able to track them down anyway? Al noticed his concerned expression and chuckled.

"Oh, it's not ordinary water. Anybody who comes into contact with water from the Lethye loses his or her memory. If Scruggs's dogs bury their noses in it, it'll throw 'em right off the scent." Edward breathed a sigh of relief. Al turned to the others and added, "Sometimes the river's water is used by the Guardians to help newly arrived mortals who had a really tough life back on Earth. It can reduce their suffering and help them face the future. It's kind of like resetting the clock, allowing them a fresh start and a way for them to make brand new memories for themselves here in the Woodbine," Al mentioned.

Edward listened as he turned his gaze back out the window. It might be nice to erase some of the painful memories of his own past.

"I hate to be nosy," Al said hesitantly, "but you folks must have done something pretty incredible to make the Jackal mad enough to risk sending his Groundlings into Guardian territory. I've never seen that many gathered together in one place so far from his Lair."

He forced a smile. "Of course, any enemies of the Jackal are friends of mine. But tell me"—his expression grew serious—"Whiplash Scruggs hasn't been seen in these parts in ages." His eyes traveled over to Edward who politely ignored his stare.

"All I'm saying is that if anybody here has aroused his special interest, well, I think somebody better tell me what's going on." He glanced at Tabitha and Mr. Spines and added, "In my experience, whenever Scruggs shows up, someone ends up dead." The stocky man looked nervous. "And it doesn't always matter whether they've already died once before or not."

Chapter Nine

MISSION

Bridgette told Al what had happened. When the boatman heard about the quest to rescue Edward's mother from the Jackal's Lair, his normally cheerful face grew even more serious.

"Breaking into the Jackal's Lair? I don't know if that's such a good idea. I heard the Jackal's got some kind of defensive shield that will rip a Guardian's wings off if they get too close." He shook his head sadly. "You're gonna need some kind of serious firepower if you want to break into that place." Al indicated Edward with a gesture of his thumb. "He looks kind of young. Does he know what he's getting into?"

"Don't worry about me," Edward said, bristling a little. "I can handle it."

"He needs training," Mr. Spines said, ignoring Edward's comment. He turned to look at Tabitha. "If you and I were to work together to give him the proper instruction, I think he can do it. The boy is special. And as far as gaining entrance to the Lair goes, even the most well fortified door has a keyhole," Spines grinned, exposing rows of his yellow, crooked teeth. "And I happen to know the one person who can make us a key. Cornelius of the Blue Snails."

"Cornelius?" Al asked, surprised. "I thought he left the Woodbine and went to the Higher Places."

"No, he just prefers to remain hidden. In fact, he's an old friend of mine," Spines replied. "Or at least he *was*, before I fell. He was the greatest smith in the Seven Worlds. He was well-known in the Higher Places for his skills at making Guardian rings."

"Are you serious? Nobody's heard from him in years," Tabitha interrupted. She looked condescendingly down at Spines. "Besides that, nobody but the highest ranking Guardians has ever *seen* one of his rings. Stories about what his amazing rings were capable of are just that, stories." She sniffed imperiously.

Tabitha glanced at Edward and smirked. "And as far as training *Edward* goes, I doubt it would work." Mr. Spines started to object, but she raised her hand to cut him off. "Unless he's a full-fledged Guardian there is no way he'd stand a chance at the Jackal's Lair. It's swarming with Groundlings as bad as Whiplash Scruggs or worse. I've been studying to be a full Guardian for fifteen years and I'm just now graduating to Guardian Third Class. At least I was, until I was ordered to go with you."

Edward noticed she delivered the last part of her statement with bitterness. Tabitha's pearly wings twitched in irritation. "There's no way a *half mortal* that can't even fly can learn what is necessary to know. He can barely speak!" She flashed Edward a haughty look and continued. "And you want me to teach him how to *sing*? Impossible!"

She's acting like I'm stupid! That was it! Edward was sick of Tabitha and her superior attitude. What Tabitha had said was partially true. He was untrained. And he understood the fact that he had absolutely no idea how to use his wings or do any of the things that Guardians could do. But he didn't care how dangerous or impossible the mission was. He was determined to find his mom and all he wanted was a chance to learn. With the blood pounding angrily in his ears, Edward stood up, trying his best to control his stutter.

"F-fine. If y-you don't want to train me, then I'll fuh-figure it out myself. I-I'm going to find her wuh-with or without your help. And i-if *he* . . ." Edward indicated Mr. Spines, ". . . s-says there's a chance if we f-find this Cornelius person then I suh-say we try it."

Edward's tall frame towered over the young Guardian and, with his ebony wings stretched out on either side of him, he looked even bigger. He was tired of people underestimating him all the time. Too much was at stake. He needed to get to his mom as soon as possible.

Emboldened by his action, Edward decided to say what he'd been feeling ever since he'd met Tabitha. And surprisingly, it came out without the slightest trace of a stutter. "I may not know much about how Guardians are supposed to behave, but you've been nothing but an arrogant snob since I've met you. In fact, come to think of it, I think you'd make a much better Groundling. All they care about are the same things you do. *Themselves*."

The color drained from Tabitha's face. The young Guardian was speechless for a full minute before she finally rose and strode out of the boatman's house, slamming the door behind her as she went.

Mr. Spines was shocked. For anyone to infer that a Guardian was acting like a Groundling was the highest of insults. But Edward had been absolutely right about Tabitha's pride. After all, nobody could recognize the symptoms better than he. Arrogance was a sticky web and the favorite of the Jackal's tools.

Had Spines been tall enough, he would have liked to pat his son on the back for his courage, but as it was, he barely came up to Edward's waist. So, on an impulse, he decided to reach out his hand toward Edward's arm, thinking to give it an encouraging squeeze.

But he wasn't prepared for Edward's reaction.

To his surprise, his son turned around at the touch, slapping his father's hand away.

"D-don't ever t-touch me," Edward said, looking furious. Mr. Spines backed away slightly, hurt.

Edward gazed down at his father with distaste. "I-I'll put up with you if it m-means finding my mom. B-but after th-that I nuh-never want to see you again."

Then Edward marched into the back bedroom of the tiny shack and slammed the door.

Once inside the tiny room, Edward flopped down on the cot. All of his triumphant feelings over his exchange with Tabitha had faded away. Now, all that was left was a shaky, sick feeling in the pit of his stomach. He didn't want to admit it to himself, but Tabitha's words had stung him deeply.

He knew it was because he'd let his guard down, mistakenly entertaining the possibility that maybe, just maybe, he'd found a place here in the Woodbine where he could finally fit in. And fit in as a Guardian, a hero.

Edward knew he had been right to defend himself, to tell Tabitha that he was going to search for his mother. But he knew he shouldn't have called her a Groundling. He had crossed a line, trying to hurt her as much as she had hurt him, and that wasn't acting like much of a Guardian, either. Maybe he was no better than her, and would have made a better Groundling himself.

He let out a deep sigh.

What did it matter anyway? Who was he kidding? He wasn't a Guardian.

As he sat at the edge of his bed, he stared out of the tiny window. The clouds had come back again, obscuring the moon from view. Right about now would have been a perfect time to calm his nerves by building a card house. But his cards were lost forever, washed away in the river of forgetfulness.

He lay back on the bed and buried his face in the pillow.

Whoever said being in the Afterlife meant it was a better life? he thought sadly.

✦ Chapter Ten ✦

SHAPE - SHIFTER

Edward didn't remember falling asleep. But the next thing he knew, Bridgette was gently shaking his shoulder to wake him.

"Huh?" he asked groggily. When he saw it was Bridgette he quickly sat up, embarrassed. Although, luckily, she didn't seem to notice that he'd been drooling. He quickly wiped the side of his mouth with the back of his hand.

"Tabitha didn't come back last night," Bridgette said. "Your fath . . . I mean *Mr. Spines* said that we'll have to go on without her."

Edward yawned. "It f-figures she didn't come back," he said matter-of-factly. "She was so f-full of herself anyway. Not a big loss if you ask me."

"Actually, it *is* a big loss," Bridgette fired back, irritated. "We really needed her. Without Tabitha we don't have any protection at all.

Your father can't sing or use his ring without the Corruption setting in again. And you're untrained and can hurt yourself if you keep randomly trying to access your powers."

She sighed. "There's only one idea I can come up with that might keep us from getting hurt while we travel to Cornelius." She took a deep breath and said, "You're going to have to learn to shape-shift."

Edward stared at her, confused. "What?"

"Shape-shift. Remake your appearance to look like what you look like on the inside. Almost all of the mortals who come to the Woodbine take on a new appearance. You're half mortal. So it's worth trying to see if you can do it."

"But wh-what if I can't?" Edward said. "I thought Guardians c-can't change the way they look?"

"*They* can't, but *you* might be different," Bridgette said encouragingly. "I think we'll just have to see what happens. You're half human. If you can change your appearance even a little bit, just enough to disguise you from Whiplash Scruggs, we might be able to travel to Cornelius without attracting attention from the Groundlings."

"B-but what about Mr. Spines? S-Scruggs could spot his porcupine quills a mile away," Edward said. "There's no possible way he wouldn't recognize him."

"Al has an old wagon he said we could use. It's pretty small, but big enough for Mr. Spines to hide in the back under a tarpaulin."

It wasn't a bad idea, and it sounded like the best plan they could manage at this point.

"I'll try it. But I d-don't get one thing," Edward said.

"Get what?" she asked.

The hurt feelings Edward had been wrestling with since the exchange with Tabitha came bubbling to the surface. Edward ran his hand through his messy hair and his wings twitched.

"W-why do y-you keep wanting to help me?" he said quietly. "Everybody else I kn-know treats m-me like I'm an idiot."

Bridgette was quiet for a moment before replying.

"I believe what my uncle said about you,

Edward. If he says that you're the Bridge Builder then he must be right. Besides," she glanced self-consciously out the window, "I don't think you're an idiot. Just because it's a little hard for you to talk sometimes doesn't mean you're not smart. I like the things you say. And I like being around you."

It was Edward's turn to feel awkward. He flushed bright crimson, flattered. Nobody that looked like Bridgette had ever liked spending time with him before.

He considered what she'd said about shape-shifting. Edward glanced down at his pale, skinny hands and his long, spindly legs. He had to admit, the prospect might be rather exciting. For as long as he could remember he'd been a little self-conscious about the way he looked. What would it be like to look like someone or something else?

Bridgette showed Edward a small book, relieving the awkward silence. "I carried this with me when we left the cottage."

Beezlenut's Guide to the Afterlife was embossed on the book's cover.

Bridgette leafed through a couple chapters, "This book is really wonderful. It lists everything a person could ever want to know about getting around in the Woodbine. It has maps, guides to great restaurants . . . all kinds of useful information. I think the Dancing Faun is even mentioned in here somewhere. It's handed out at the docks when people first come here." She glanced up at Edward, "You would have received one but you didn't arrive here in the traditional way."

Then Bridgette found the chapter she was looking for. Edward looked over her shoulder as she read.

"The Soul Made Flesh" was the title.

She scanned the page until she came to the passage she was looking for. "Aha, here it is," she said. "I did this so long ago, I forgot the words."

Edward wondered what Bridgette looked like before she'd arrived in the Woodbine. He couldn't imagine her looking any different than she did now, with her curling, auburn hair and beautiful, dark eyes.

"All right. The first thing you have to do is to

concentrate on whatever it is that you think you really look like," Bridgette said. She gave him an encouraging look. "For most people there can be an assortment of choices, but on some basic level, anything you choose has to be an aspect of who you are. For example I," she indicated herself with a gesture, "tried being a giant pigeon and a walking tree before I settled on this body," she said smiling. "I could see myself as any of those things, but this body was the one that felt the most comfortable. And well . . . it's pretty different than I looked when I left Earth . . ."

Edward noticed the hesitation in her voice. "I bet you were always beautiful," he said, trying to reassure her. He was glad the words had come out without a stutter.

"Does that really matter?" Bridgette snapped. She looked really angry. Her reaction caught him completely off guard.

"Uh, n-n-nuh-no," he stammered, his face getting red. "I j-juh-juh-juh-juh . . ."

". . . Just thought that I had an easy life because I was so pretty back on Earth. Well, you have no idea what it was like for me back there."

Edward couldn't figure out what he'd done wrong. He'd just been trying to be nice.

He quickly tried to salvage the situation. Bridgette was the closest thing he'd had to a friend as long as he could remember. "L-listen, I'm sorry okay? I d-didn't mean to make you feel bad," he said, cursing his stutter. "P-puh-please forgive me, all right? I didn't mean anything by it."

Edward waited nervously for her to respond. After a moment, Bridgette glanced up at him with a softened expression. "Oh, let's just forget it," she said. "It's not worth getting into . . . let's get back to your appearance."

She skimmed the instructions.

"All you have to do is concentrate on who you think you really are deep inside and then say the words written here."

She handed him the book. Edward looked at the page and read the words, *Metageitnios tarantinarcheo.*

It was a mouthful. And for him to try to say anything that elaborate without stuttering was a daunting task.

But Edward had to at least try. He

concentrated, trying to imagine what his inner self should look like. He closed his eyes, his mind racing to figure out what it might be. Different images flashed through his head. He would like to be big and strong, with thick arms and a handsome face. He'd seen a picture once of a circus strongman. But somehow he knew that wasn't right. Even though he'd like to look like that, something inside of him knew it wasn't really who he was.

He thought some more and, just when he thought he might not be able to come up with anything, a picture flashed in his mind. It was of an illustration from a book of fairy tales his mother had read him when he was very young.

A huge grin spread across his face as he thought about that.

"Sooplemex," he said, not realizing he was speaking aloud.

"What?" Bridgette asked.

"Oh, i-it's a cuh-character in a fairy tale my m-mom used to tell me about. H-he was a winged leopard," Edward said, looking embarrassed.

Bridgette giggled. Then she noticed Edward's stricken expression and quickly added, "Oh, I'm not laughing at you. I think it's a great idea! I'm only laughing because I think it's the first time I've seen you look really happy." She glanced at him shyly and added, "It's really nice to see your smile, Edward."

Edward smiled again and studied the magic words more closely. He had to sound them out verbally in his head a few times before he felt ready to say them. After a moment, he pictured the image of a flying leopard clearly in his mind. Then, after taking a deep breath, he recited the words in the book.

"*Metageitnios tarantinarcheo.*"

To his surprise, he said the words without a single stutter.

Seconds later, a strange, fluttering sensation began in the pit of his stomach. It started like a soft tickle and then grew into a powerful, burning feeling. The hair on his arms began to thicken into golden fur. He watched, stunned, as his fingers shrunk, becoming powerful paws. His whole body gave a shudder and his bones creaked, feeling like they were being compressed inside of a gigantic vise.

Then, just seconds after it had begun, the transformation was complete.

"Did it work?" he asked expectantly. But he could immediately tell by Bridgette's expression that something had gone wrong. She was staring at him with a mix of compassion and something else. Was it disgust?

"H-how d-duh-do I look?" he stuttered.

"Well," she said awkwardly, "I don't know if it's exactly what you were picturing. Maybe I better get a mirror so you can see for yourself."

Edward waited while Bridgette ran into the other room. She returned a moment later with a small hand mirror. He raised it up to his face nervously.

The face that stared back at him was definitely not Sooplemex's. In fact, it was something else entirely.

"At least it kind of worked," Bridgette said. She tried to sound optimistic.

Edward just stared at the face looking back at him in the glass and groaned. In all the years of feeling self-conscious about his appearance, never in a million years would he have ever thought he could have found a way to look worse.

✦ Chapter Eleven ✦
LEAVING THE BOATMAN

Edward followed Bridgette back into the main room, dreading everyone's reaction to his new appearance.

"What's that thing?" Al said, jumping back a pace.

"It's Edward," Bridgette replied soothingly. "He's just changed a little bit."

"You call that a little?" the boatman said. He whistled through his teeth. "Son, you better be careful walking around town looking like that. Folks might mistake you for a Groundling."

Edward scowled. It was the same thing he'd thought when he'd first caught sight of himself in the mirror. Instead of a majestic leopard with large, golden wings, he looked like a freakish mix of an animal and a human. He had something resembling a leopard's broad, flat nose, except it was covered with pinkish skin. Horrible black spots stretched from his forehead to his chin and his eyes were irregular, one looked like a cat's and one like his own brown one. His teeth were pointed, just like a cat's, only smaller, giving him that characteristic Groundling smile that he'd come to hate so much.

All in all, he looked like a terrific mess.

He couldn't help glancing at Mr. Spines, who looked hurriedly away. But what Edward spotted in that brief exchange was an understanding expression. His father knew all about what it was like to live in a body that was tragically malformed.

"C-can I just change b-back?" Edward said. His tongue moved in his mouth awkwardly, unused to its new, animal palette. His voice was almost a growl. But unfortunately, he still had his stutter.

"The book says that you'll have to wait six hours before you can transform again," Bridgette said, examining the text. "But the good news is that by then we'll have traveled out of the nearby towns and should be able to stick to the country.

Your disguise, as er . . . odd . . . as it might be, will at least help us get to the open roads."

Mr. Spines cleared his throat. Then he said, "The girl's right. And we have no time to waste. After we're far enough away and you can transform back, I'll begin your training myself. You'll have to learn the mastery of the ring, your wings, and the Songs. I'll teach you all that I'm able to on our way to Cornelius's Valley. It would have been nice to have Tabitha to help with your flight instruction, but I can teach you the basic principles." Spines hesitated for a moment, and then added, "That is, if you want me to."

Edward didn't reply immediately. Although he knew that it was important to learn the new skills, he still had a hard time being around his father. He felt bad for snapping at him the night before. Somewhere deep inside, he knew that Mr. Spines had just been trying to be friendly. But Edward wasn't ready to forgive his father for what he'd done, for all that he'd put Edward and his mother through.

Finally, after a long pause, Edward nodded slowly.

"Right," Mr. Spines said, straightening up. "Time for us to go."

Al sent them off with a cheery wave and a basket filled with provisions for the road ahead. They all thanked him for his generosity as they set out, promising to return the little pony that he'd lent them to pull the wagon.

They traveled up from the boatman's shack into the nearby forest. The Seven Bridges Road began there.

Mr. Spines was going to wait to hide under the tarpaulin until they came in sight of the first city. He spoke up from where he sat in the back of the wagon when the signpost passed by. He said, "This is the old road, the main thoroughfare through the Woodbine. We'll be traveling this for several miles until we cross the border where the Woodbine ends and the Blighted Lands begin. That's the official demarcation point of the Jackal's territory."

"I thought Cornelius's Valley was in the Woodbine," Bridgette said.

"He lives just over the border," Spines replied. "It's because of the Baruch that he's able to protect himself in that hostile territory."

"W-what's a Baruch?" Edward asked.

Spines noticed that Edward was being slightly more friendly. Glad that they were on semi-civil terms, Spines replied, "They're battle snails— terrifically huge beasts with blue shells and faces that look almost human. They're some of the oldest inhabitants of the Woodbine and are said to have existed before the Guardians were created."

"I've only read about them in fairy books, like *The Bridges Between the Worlds,*" Bridgette confessed. "I never even believed that Cornelius was real until you mentioned him last night.

Edward scratched an itch on his leg with a furry paw. The partial transformation was really uncomfortable. His fur felt hot and itchy and the eye that looked like a cat's focused differently than his human eye. His old body never looked so good to him as it did at that moment. Trying to distract himself from his discomfort, he asked to nobody in particular, "What city do we have to go through before we're on the open road?"

Bridgette replied, "Woodhaven. It's a really interesting place. Many of the newly arrived mortals settle there, hoping to reunite with loved ones. Be prepared," she warned Edward with a smile. "You'll probably be asked a dozen times if you are a long lost relative of someone."

Edward wondered if anyone in the city would want to believe they knew him. He looked so strange and frightening that he doubted anyone would think he'd willingly chosen to look like he did!

Bridgette added, "I just remembered something! There's a big carnival going on in Woodhaven this week," her face broke into a wide smile. "This is great! You'll love it! They've got some amazing things to see."

Mr. Spines broke in. "We shouldn't delay for a carnival. We need to get to Cornelius's Valley as soon as possible. And the sooner we can get out of the city, the sooner we can start Edward's training."

But Edward, who was thinking that a carnival might be just what he needed to lift his spirits, spoke up in Bridgette's defense.

"We d-don't have to stay long. I wuh-want to see it."

Bridgette smiled up at Edward, and the matter was settled. After all, Mr. Spines would be hiding in the back of the wagon while Bridgette drove. It wasn't like he had much choice.

Edward ignored his father's grumbles as the little wagon made its way along the muddy road, deeper and deeper into the forest. Because of the recent rain, the wonderfully clean scent of pine needles and fresh earth was in the air. It smelled like Oregon.

Edward couldn't wait to see his mother again. Maybe they could start over with a nice little house here in the Woodbine, just like they had back home, surrounded by pine trees.

As the trees thinned, Edward could make out the waving banners of a city in the distance. It looked a little bit like a rustic fort.

Bridgette nudged the pony into a trot and called back over her shoulder, "Better get down, Mr. Spines. There are some guards up ahead." She squinted into the distance, eyeing the sentries. The tough-looking men seemed to be involved in some kind of major disturbance at the city gates. "And it looks like something's wrong."

Chapter Twelve

WOODHAVEN

"Whatever you do, don't mention your real name," Edward heard Spines hiss from underneath the tarp. "We don't want anyone in Woodhaven to know our business or who we are, understand?"

Edward nodded. As the city drew closer, Edward could make out sentries, dressed in cavalry uniforms with sweeping feathers perched on broad-brimmed hats. A large crowd was trying to edge past a couple of individuals who were involved in a fight just inside the massive log gates.

The sentries were trying to separate the brawlers, but were having a difficult time. Edward quickly saw the reason why. It wasn't two mortals fighting. It was a pair of Guardians!

"By the Seven Bridges, Gadreel! I won't allow

you to do it!" one of the Guardians thundered. He was big and lantern-jawed, and had the other one, Edward assumed it was "Gadreel," pinned to the ground, holding him in place with a knee on his neck.

The wiry Guardian on the ground reacted, quickly grabbing a handful of dust and flinging it into his opponent's eyes. The bigger Guardian stumbled backward and Gadreel leaped up. In a swift movement he grabbed the other's arm and gave it a ferocious twist. There was a sound like wood splintering and the bigger Guardian cried out in pain.

The Guardian grinned as his bigger opponent slumped to the ground, his hawklike face alight with triumph.

"Too late, Kyriel!" he screeched. "I've joined with the Jackal! Not even Mi'kael can stop me now!"

The two sentries leaped at the wiry Guardian, but were flung backward with a single word. The stunned mortals thudded against the log gates, unconscious. The crowd around the fighting Guardians scattered, giving them a wide berth.

It was obvious that the crowd had never seen a fight like this before.

"You fool!" Kyriel shouted between clenched teeth. The Guardian was gripping his broken arm and seemed to be in a great deal of pain. "For the sake of our father, don't go through with it. Break your contract!"

Gadreel withdrew an Oroborus and shouted the word Edward had heard the Groundlings shout on the riverbank.

"NSH!"

The ring burst into a circle of red flame. The thin, sharp-faced Guardian strode over to where his brother knelt on the ground.

"You're the fool, Kyriel. Following father's orders like a mindless drone," he gestured at the assorted crowd. "You're hardly better than they are. Stupid sheep without a shepherd," he mocked. "You'd spend your whole life protecting this lot?" Gadreel's eyes burned with malice. "I told you not to interfere with my Charges, brother. They were *my* business, not yours."

"You were inspiring them to hate. You gave them weapons, goading them to kill! That's not what Guardians *do*, Gadreel. I had to get involved or they would have murdered each other. Is that what you intended?"

"You humiliated me in front of father," Gadreel hissed. "I was going to be demoted in front of the entire Council. I couldn't allow it."

Bridgette whispered to Edward, "I don't believe it! Those are Mi'kael's sons. They're two of the most powerful Guardians in the army!"

Edward heard a rustle and noticed Mr. Spines staring out from a tiny hole in the canvas cover. There was a sharp intake of breath as he recognized the two brothers.

"Gadreel's going to kill him," Spines whispered suddenly. "You must put a stop to it, Edward. Here, take this." There was a slight scurrying sound and the next thing Edward knew Spines had shoved the wedding band from his left hand into Edward's palm.

"W-what do I do with it?" Edward stammered.

"This was made for me by Cornelius. It is one of the most powerful rings left in the Woodbine. You must stare into the center of the ring and empty your mind. Then, with as much focus as you can muster, I want you to say *Qados* as loud and as clear as you can," Spines said.

"But I-I can't . . ."

"You MUST," Spines hissed. "Kyriel is a vital part of the Guardian army. He provides his father with reconnaissance on the Jackal's activities. If killed, it will be a major victory for the Jackal and a heavy blow to the Guardians. You must stop him!"

Edward was frightened. He had no idea if he could do it. What if he couldn't?

But Edward knew that if he wanted to be a hero, a real Guardian, then he had to at least try. His furry, leopard paw shook nervously as he raised the tiny ring to his good eye. He tried to concentrate, staring into the center of it, just as Mr. Spines had told him to. But so many anxious thoughts were racing through his mind, that he couldn't find a way to blank them out.

Outside the Woodhaven gate, Kyriel reached for his Guardian's ring with his one good arm. But it wasn't there.

There was a murmur in the crowd, causing Edward to glance up from the wedding ring. It was then that Edward realized how Mr. Spines had known what Gadreel was intending to do. The ever-observant Spines had seen Kyriel's smooth ring hanging from Gadreel's belt before Kyriel knew it was missing.

Gadreel grinned mockingly at his brother. "Too slow, my brother. Much too slow. You really are quite overrated in your abilities, Kyriel. I've been telling the Council for years they should have chosen me to be the espionage agent, not you."

The flaming Oroborus that Gadreel held seemed to burn with renewed vigor. "Good-bye, brother," Gadreel said icily. "Your wings will make an excellent trophy in the Jackal's chambers."

"*Qados!*"

As soon as Edward had said the word, the tiny ring had grown, becoming a large, flaming hoop of blue fire. Now the boy stood, trembling, with it clutched tightly in his furry fist.

"Throw it, NOW!" Spines hissed.

Whether it was by accident or by luck, Edward's throw was true. He'd reacted without thinking, hurling the ring with all of his might at Gadreel.

The Guardian hadn't been expecting an attack, especially not one from someone who looked nothing like a Guardian, but he reacted faster than anyone expected. With a lightning-fast downward flap from his wings, he shot into the air. At the same time, he whipped his hand around and deflected Mr. Spines's ring with his Oroborus, sending it hurtling back toward Edward.

Edward had no idea what to do. Mr. Spines's blazing ring was racing toward him and he didn't know whether to duck or to try to catch it! At the last minute he decided ducking was the best idea and dove from the cart to the earth, barely avoiding being hit.

Mr. Spines's ring missed him and hurtled into the forest behind them, its blue flames igniting a few of the pine branches as it disappeared into the woods.

Gadreel landed lightly on the ground next to Edward, who was still lying in the dirt. The fallen Guardian cackled as he took a closer look at Edward's misshapen form. "What's this? A mortal with a ring? Now I've seen everything," he said with a sneer.

Edward rose awkwardly to his feet, giving everyone a good look at his misshapen form.

"Well, mortal. You must possess the ugliest soul I've ever seen," Gadreel smiled cruelly. "And for a wretched, deformed creature like you to have the audacity to attack me, well, that's just unacceptable." Gadreel's voice lowered into a sneer, "I don't know how you did it, ugly one. But it certainly won't ever happen again."

"Leave him alone, Gadreel!" Kyriel called out. The big Guardian had risen to his feet. In spite of his badly broken arm, Edward thought he still looked formidable. "If you harm him, you'll answer to me."

Gadreel let out a long, angry laugh. "Oh, I'll take my chances, brother. Besides, I've got friends now. Friends of power and influence that have little regard for you, or your precious *Council*."

There was a parting in the crowd behind Gadreel and, to Edward's horror, Whiplash

Scruggs, flanked on either side by Henry and Lilith Asmoday, stepped out of the crowd.

Edward's heart stopped for a moment as Scruggs looked him up and down. But then the massive Groundling turned back to Gadreel, with no hint of recognition. Edward's disguise had worked!

Scruggs, Henry, and Lilith seemed eager to see Gadreel prove himself in front of his brother. Kyriel glared at the assembled Groundlings. In spite of his broken arm and being hopelessly outnumbered, the Guardian looked like he was going to try and fight.

Gadreel turned his attention back to Edward. "Now then, where was I?"

Gadreel grinned and raised his flaming Oroborus. This was *it*. Edward was finally going to discover what happens when someone dies in the Afterlife. He'd first wondered about it when he'd arrived and almost drowned in a river. He was curious about it, but he really hadn't wanted to find out firsthand. But there was nothing he could do now. He just stood where he was, his body trembling as the evil Guardian prepared to throw.

Let it be quick, he prayed.

Suddenly, something flashed downward from over Edward's left shoulder. A sizzling ring smashed into Gadreel's Oroborus, sending it spinning out of reach. A blur of wings followed close behind and a loud voice called out, *"Magen!"*

There was a burst of white light as Gadreel was thrown backward, smashing into Whiplash Scruggs, Henry, and Lilith. The three Groundlings toppled where they stood, scattering panicked mortals in their wake.

It was Tabitha!

The Guardian caught her returning ring with lightning reflexes and then, with a mighty heave, hurled it at Gadreel again. As she threw, Edward caught a snatch of a melody that he'd never heard before. But to his surprise, he recognized the words she was singing. He'd used them before, when he'd tried to escape from the cellar beneath the Foundry. They had come to him unexpectedly, as if they were a long forgotten memory.

Azru Li . . . Azru Li . . . Azru Li.

Tabitha made a perfect, deadly throw.

In one terrific slice, the blazing ring made contact with the base of Gadreel's outstretched wings, severing them from his shoulders.

The wail that filled the air around them was terrible, echoing from the trees, air, and earth itself. The ground beneath Edward's feet shook and several mortals fell to the ground.

There was the briefest outline of Gadreel's tortured form. And then, seconds later, the Guardian was gone, dissolving into nothing.

Edward stared at the spot, a terrified expression on his face.

So that's what happens if you die in the Afterlife.

Chapter Thirteen

A NARROW ESCAPE

"Go!" Tabitha shouted to Bridgette.

"Edward, get in the cart!" Bridgette called. Edward rushed over to the waiting wagon. At the mention of Edward's name, Whiplash Scruggs rose from where he'd been knocked down, his eyes widening in surprise.

"Get the boy!" Lilith screeched, finally recognizing her prey in spite of his disguise. Scruggs and Henry Asmoday rushed toward the wagon, their sharp teeth bared.

They moved so quickly, Bridgette barely had time to react. She slapped the reins down hard on the little pony's back. But just as the wagon pulled forward, Edward felt a powerful, vise-like grip on his wrist, nearly jerking him from his seat.

"Got you, boy!" Scruggs shouted. The familiar, Kentucky drawl made Edward shiver.

Suddenly a small, prickly body leapt from underneath the tarp and pounced on Scrugg's meaty back. Then the creature bit deeply into Scruggs' shoulder with his broken, yellow teeth.

"Aaaaaiiiieeee!" Scruggs cried, releasing his grip on Edward's arm. The pony shot forward, nearly throwing Edward and Bridgette from the cart. As the wagon raced away, Edward turned back to see Tabitha, Spines, and Kyriel fighting the enemy.

"I–I've got to go back!" Edward shouted. He couldn't let Tabitha or Mr. Spines die after they had just saved his life.

"No! We have to get away. You're too important!" Bridgette exclaimed.

"Why?" he shouted back.

"Because you're the Bridge Builder!"

At that moment Edward realized that Bridgette really believed that prophecy. He wasn't some legendary figure. Even though he wanted to be, he still wasn't even a Guardian yet.

His heart sank as he glanced back to where Mr. Spines and Tabitha were fighting. Some hero. If he was something special, wouldn't he have gone back and rescued them in spite of anything Bridgette said? But he couldn't bring himself to do it. He had no idea what he could do. Edward still couldn't believe what Mr. Spines had done, risking his life for him.

Bridgette continued to goad the pony forward as far as the little beast could carry them. Her face was pale and resolute, and she looked desperate to get as far away from the Groundlings as possible.

After several hours the pine forest gave way to rolling green hills dotted with twisted oak trees. As the shadows on the ground lengthened, they finally slowed the cart, reasonably sure that they had escaped.

Bridgette eased the wagon off into a thicket by the side of the road. Both she and Edward were quiet as they unhooked the wagon from the pony and led it to a grassy area to be rubbed down.

Several minutes passed in silence as they made camp. Then, as Edward was digging through the supplies in the back of the wagon, Bridgette suddenly spoke, interrupting his morose thoughts.

"It's been six hours," she said. "We can change you back to your old appearance now."

Bridgette handed him the *Beezlenut's Guide to the Afterlife*, and Edward immediately turned to the page that dealt with transformations. He didn't want to wait another second to be himself again.

He reviewed the strange words in the book, just to be safe. Then he concentrated, imagining himself the way he always appeared. Edward spoke the words and after the strange sensation of feeling like his bones were all pushed out of joint, was pleased to find himself restored to his old, gangly self. He ran his thin fingers through his mop of black hair and over his skinny face. He even flexed his disheveled wings, and sighed happily.

It had never felt so good to be in his own body.

There was plenty of firewood beneath one of the larger oak trees. Edward gathered as much as he could, toting it over to the spot that Bridgette had indicated would be a good place for a fire.

"Here's the w-wood," Edward said.

Bridgette was standing several feet away from the place she'd cleared and ringed with large stones. Edward set the wood down in the middle of the ring, unsure of what to do next.

"There're matches in the back of the wagon," Bridgette said in a flat voice.

"Is everything all right?" Edward asked, noticing her tone.

"Yes," she said. But Edward could tell that everything wasn't all right. She was staring at the center of the ring, lost in her private thoughts. Even though Edward had never built a fire before, he could tell that the task was going to be left up to him. He sighed and walked over to the wagon, and, after a couple minutes of searching, found the matches.

Edward guessed that Bridgette must be worried about Tabitha and Spines. Maybe the fight had affected her more deeply than he realized.

After several burnt matches, Edward finally got the first spark to appear. Bridgette sat several feet away with her arms hugging her knees, staring into the flames.

"Why d-don't you come closer?" he asked conversationally. "It's really warm."

Bridgette shook her head.

"How come?" he asked. "What's the m-matter?"

"I can't talk about it."

"Are you s-sure? I'm a g-good listener," Edward said. He could tell that something was really bothering her. She'd always been so helpful and encouraging to him, he wanted to return the favor.

After a few seconds, Bridgette took a deep breath. She gave Edward an intense look. "If I tell you about something, do you promise to keep it a secret? I've only told two other people since I arrived here and that was Jack and Joyce."

Edward nodded. "I promise."

Bridgette took a deep breath. "It's . . . it's about something that happened to me back on Earth. "Two years ago there was . . . an *accident* at my house. My parents had gone out, leaving me to babysit my little sister, Katie."

Bridgette reached into the pocket of her jacket and withdrew a small, black-and-white photograph. She handed it to Edward. He stared down at a girl close to his own age with her smiling parents and a little baby.

To his surprise, the girl in the picture looked exactly like the Bridgette he knew here in the Woodbine. He was wrong about his suspicions about her looking different back on Earth. She looked the same!

The baby in the photograph looked to be about a year old and was smiling widely, dimples dotting each of her chubby cheeks.

Edward stared at the picture as Bridgette continued her story.

"We didn't have electricity at my house. We used kerosene lamps." She looked up at Edward with a hollow expression. "Katie and I were playing in the living room. I was swinging her around and we were laughing . . ." Bridgette's chin began to quiver, and Edward could tell she was trying very hard not to cry. "My arm hit the lamp near the window. It spilled kerosene everywhere. The whole house caught on fire. By the time my parents got there, it was too late. Katie was gone, and I . . ."

Tears were streaming down Bridgette's cheeks. She didn't say anything else for a long moment.

Edward moved closer and tentatively laid his hand on her shoulder. When Bridgette could finally speak again, her voice was thick with emotion.

"K-Katie went straight to the Higher Places, of course. All babies do, you know," she sniffed. "But I didn't die. My face and body were badly burned and the doctors said I might never wake up," her voice trailed to a whisper.

"I don't understand," Edward said. "You m-mean you're not dead?"

"I'm in a coma," Bridgette said quietly. "But they don't think I'll live much longer."

Edward didn't know what to say. It was hard to believe that the same Bridgette, full of life and sitting right next to him, was also on Earth dying in a hospital.

He thought about what her parents must be feeling and felt tears in his own eyes. So that was why she reacted so strongly when he'd mentioned how pretty she was. She had been beautiful once, but wasn't any longer. And she must miss her family so much—definitely as much as he missed his mother.

Bridgette glanced up at him with tear-stained cheeks. "Sometimes I can hear what the doctors say down there, even though I'm here. If I die, like they're saying I will, then there's only one thing I want to do. I want to travel the Seven Bridges up to the Higher Places so that I can see my sister again. That's how I knew I was supposed to come with you back at my uncle's house."

She looked up at him meaningfully. "I knew I was supposed to help you become the Bridge Builder. I knew it just as soon as Uncle Jack finished the story about you and your family." She looked down at the ground, staring at the place between her shoes.

"I know how terrible my parents feel, the guilt they feel for not being home when the fire happened. Even though I know it was my fault for breaking the lamp, they blame themselves for going out that night instead of staying home. I know how much they suffer, because I can hear them in my head every day, talking about it in the hospital room."

Edward could see just how difficult that was for Bridgette. She was carrying a burden much too heavy for anyone her age.

"But that's just because your parents love you. That's w-why they feel so badly. Maybe if they w-would have stayed home the fire wouldn't have happened, but they didn't know that. Everybody m-makes mistakes," he said reassuringly.

Bridgette nodded her head slowly and said, "That's exactly right, Edward. And it's why I wanted to tell you my story. I know that you hate your father for what he did when he signed the contract with the Jackal. But, just like my parents, he can't forgive himself either. He made a terrible mistake and has been trying to fix it ever since. He loves you, Edward."

As much as Edward wanted someone to blame his frustrations on, he couldn't deny that what Bridgette said was true.

His father had sacrificed himself so that he and Bridgette could get away. Back on Earth, he'd rescued Edward from Whiplash Scruggs and again from Asmoday and Lilith. His father had tried to hide him as a baby. Even though he had signed a contract with the Jackal, he'd done everything in his power to break it.

Edward's vision grew blurry and he turned away so that Bridgette wouldn't see him cry. He quickly wiped a sleeve across his face and cleared his throat awkwardly. Bridgette placed her warm, small hand inside Edward's own. They sat there in silence with their backs to the fire for several moments, staring outward at the shadowy hills. It felt good to let go of the resentment he'd been carrying ever since he found out that Mr. Spines was his father.

Suddenly a movement in the shadows caught Edward's attention.

"Bridgette . . ." Edward whispered. The girl turned to see where Edward was pointing. Her eyes grew wide and they both stood up, staring anxiously at the approaching shadow.

"Quick, get behind me," Edward said, balling up his fists.

"What are you going to do?" Bridgette asked, sounding afraid.

"Just get back. If it's Scruggs I'm going to say that Word of Power again." Edward steadied himself. "When I do, you run and get the pony. It's our only chance."

"No, don't," Bridgette warned. "You could really hurt yourself . . ."

But before she finished her sentence, the figure revealed itself by the light of the campfire. Both Edward and Bridgette gasped.

Tabitha limped toward them, her face and arms covered with burns and deep scratches. Her wings were tattered in several places.

Edward and Bridgette rushed forward to help her. They settled her next to the fire.

"I tried to stop them, but I couldn't. They were too strong," Tabitha said in a weak voice, her large, green eyes turned to Edward.

Her voice faltered. Edward watched as her eyes filled with tears. Edward didn't know what to do. He'd never seen Tabitha like this. She'd always seemed so self-assured. So confident.

"Edward . . ." she said in a plaintive whisper. "They took your father."

Chapter Fourteen

PURPOSE

"I'm not going to let them keep him," Edward said grimly. He knelt down beside Tabitha and examined her wounds. Her face was badly scratched and her hair had been singed on one side. Tears streamed down her face.

"You need help," Edward said solemnly.

"I'll be okay, they're just scratches," she said, wiping away some of her tears. Then she looked up at Edward and added, "I was wrong, you know. It wasn't right for me to treat you the way I did. I resented you because I was supposed to be promoted the night we met at Jack's house. There was a ceremony planned at the Council chamber and all I could think of at the time was how angry I was that I was going to miss it."

Tabitha's voice softened.

"I can see now that it wasn't as important as

I thought it was. You were right Edward. I was
acting arrogant and selfish. I think that's why my
master sent me on this mission. I don't think I
was ready to be promoted."

She looked genuinely sorry. "I hope you can
forgive me. A true Guardian wouldn't have acted
like I did."

Edward nodded, feeling awkward. "Of
c-course I f-forgive you. But the s-same thing
goes for me. I sh-shouldn't have called you a
Groundling."

They really smiled at each other for the first
time since they'd met. Then Tabitha said, "Your
father asked me to train you and I'll do it. To
be perfectly honest, I don't know if you're the
Bridge Builder or not. But I did see how you
handled yourself against those Groundlings at
Woodhaven. For someone with no idea of how to
use a ring, you threw well."

She reached into a small pouch on her blue
sash. Then she held out her palm, offering
something to Edward. He looked at the slim,
golden circle that rested on her hand.

It was his father's wedding ring.

"You'll need this," she said.

"You found it!" Edward cried, taking the ring. As he gazed at it he noticed an inscription inside of the band.

He moved closer to the fire to get a better look. The words were tiny, but printed in simple block letters.

Melchior and Sarah. Love never fails.

Edward's eyes burned. The inscription was so simple but the words were powerful. They echoed over and over in his mind. *Love never fails. Love NEVER fails.*

His father was sorry. He'd made mistakes that Edward could forgive. When he'd chosen to fall he'd risked everything to be with Edward's mother and even though he'd gone about it in the wrong way, it had taken a tremendous act of sacrifice. Suddenly Edward knew something that both he and his father had in common. Something he'd never realized before.

They both loved his mother.

He glanced back at Tabitha. "And I m-might not know how to sing one of those H-Healing Songs yet," he said. "But at least I can help with s-some bandages. We need to get you f-fixed up as soon as we can. Only you can teach me the thing I want to learn first."

"And what's that?" asked Tabitha.

He smiled.

"To fly."

Chapter Fifteen

PURSUIT

"Oh, my back!" Bridgette moaned. She stretched, and winced at her protesting muscles. "That was the longest night of my life."

"You should have come closer to the fire," Tabitha said.

Bridgette didn't reply. Instead she set about gathering a few things for breakfast. The three had slept through the chilly night on blankets from the wagon. Edward and Tabitha had the advantage of wings, which had acted both as a second blanket and a mattress. But Bridgette had spent a miserable night huddled a considerable distance from the fire. Because of his promise to Bridgette not to say anything about her story, Edward hadn't told Tabitha the reason why.

"Wh-when do you want to s-start my training?" Edward asked Tabitha eagerly.

She smiled. "We need a nice area with plenty of space—preferably a hilltop."

"How long do you think it will take to train Edward?" Bridgette asked. She looked anxious as she handed out the contents from a basket that Al had packed. Edward thanked Bridgette and unwrapped the waxed paper from a small packet and found a delicious looking ham sandwich and a hard-boiled egg inside.

"Hard to say," said Tabitha, unwinding the bandages from her wings. "Some students are quicker than others." She gave her wings an experimental flex and the feathers flared out in response. Tabitha winced a little, still feeling the effects of yesterday's battle.

"I'm just worried about getting to Cornelius's Valley without being discovered," Bridgette admitted.

"I'm not sure we can get there. Only Melchior knew exactly where it was. We haven't any kind of map," Tabitha replied.

"He said it w-was over the border in the J-Jackal's territory," Edward mentioned.

"Yes, but that could be anywhere," Bridgette

said. "The Woodbine is huge."

"She's right," Tabitha added. "I wouldn't know the first place to begin looking. Until yesterday, I thought Cornelius of the Blue Snails was just a legend. Even now, I'm not so sure."

Edward frowned. There had to be a way to find Cornelius. His father had said that Cornelius could provide them with a key that would get them into the Jackal's Lair. Suddenly an idea came to him.

"What about my father's w-workshop?" Edward asked excitedly. "He muh-mentioned that his apprentices S-Sariel and Artemis were hidden there. Maybe they'll know about it."

Tabitha brightened. "That's possible. It's not far from here. When I was a cherub, my instructor took a group of us there during a music history class. It was pretty run down, but you could tell that it had once been magnificent."

"I really want to see it," Edward said. Learning more about who his father had been before his fall had suddenly become more important to him. What kind of a Guardian had he been?

"Sounds good to me," Bridgette said. "I don't feel safe here." She gazed at the brown, rolling hills around them. If Groundlings were looking for them, they wouldn't be hard to spot. The thicket where they'd set up camp was the most obvious place to hide. Everything else was open grass dotted with the occasional oak tree.

"Let me check to make sure nobody's around," Tabitha said after swallowing a bite of sandwich. Edward studied her movement as she spread her wings and crouched. A second later, she was flying above the trees.

Edward stared after her, watching until she was a tiny, black dot against the brilliant blue sky. She made it look so effortless! Would it be possible for him to do what she could do? Twenty minutes later, Tabitha landed gracefully at the edge of the thicket. She gritted her teeth against the pain as she hit the ground.

"Are y-you okay?" Edward stammered.

Tabitha nodded, her face pale. "Two troops of Groundlings," Tabitha said breathlessly. "One was heading south. I have a feeling they're busy delivering Melchior to the Jackal. But the other is heading in our direction. They're only about a mile away and Scruggs is with them."

"Then wuh-we should fight!" Edward said, trying to sound braver than he felt. In spite of his fear of Scruggs, he was sick of running away. He couldn't erase the image of his father risking his life when he attacked Scruggs so that Edward could escape.

Tabitha shook her head gently. "I admire your courage, Edward. But we're in no condition to take on a whole troop of Groundlings."

"Then what should we do?" Bridgette asked anxiously. "If we stay here, they'll find us!"

Tabitha looked grave. "There's not much we can do. Groundling trackers are relentless. Once they have our scent, they'll follow us wherever we go."

"Isn't there any way w-we can throw them off?" Edward asked. "You know, l-luh-like we did at the Lethye?"

Tabitha thought for a moment. "We'd never make it back to the river in time. They'd capture us before we were even close. There's only one possible way I can think of that might work, but it would be incredibly dangerous."

"What is it?" Bridgette asked eagerly.

Tabitha paused. For the first time, Edward saw fear written on her features. She bit her lip and gazed at them with a hollow-eyed expression.

"It's a place even the Groundlings fear. Specter's Hollow."

✦ Chapter Sixteen ✦
SPECTER'S HOLLOW

"Specter's Hollow? You can't be serious!"
Bridgette exclaimed. She looked horrified.

"It's the only way," Tabitha said miserably,
clearly afraid.

"But which is worse?" Bridgette asked. "I
never thought I'd say it, but maybe being taken to
the Jackal is better. At least then we'd know what
we're up against."

Edward gazed at both of them, looking
confused. "I d-don't understand. What are you
guys talking about?" He couldn't imagine any
place being worse than the Jackal's Lair.

"It's the place where people go if they die
here in the Afterlife. It doesn't matter if you're
a Guardian, Groundling, or mortal. Even the
Jackal, if he's ever killed, will have to go there.
My uncle Jack told me that Specter's Hollow is

the place where a person faces his or her deepest fears. Those who can't find the courage to move past them are often trapped there for eternity, endlessly facing the most terrible things they can imagine," Bridgette explained.

Tabitha nodded, adding, "The beings in Specter's Hollow are often what mortals on Earth refer to as 'poltergeists.' The people there are hopelessly trapped in an 'in-between' place, both haunting and being haunted."

Edward shuddered. It sounded like a terrible place!

Tabitha removed the golden ring from her belt. She gripped its edges and looked purposefully into its center. "*Mavet*," she said in a firm voice. Edward watched as the ring grew in circumference, becoming large enough for the three of them to walk through. Inside the center of the ring the air shimmered and swirled with magical energy. Edward had seen Mr. Spines do the same thing once with his ring back on Earth. He'd forgotten that a Guardian's ring could be used both as a weapon and as a transportation device.

"Hey, couldn't we j-just use your ring to take us somewhere other than Specter's H-Hollow?" Edward said eagerly. Why hadn't he thought of it before? After all, Spines *had* used his to help them escape Whiplash Scruggs back on Earth. But his excitement faded when Tabitha shook her head.

"I can't," she said sadly. "I haven't been taught how to do it yet. The Hollow is the only place apprentices are allowed to learn. The other portals are reserved for Higher Ranks."

Bridgette bit her fingernail, looking worried. "I don't want to go. I-I don't think I can do it," she said. Edward had never seen her look so terrified. He moved close and gently took her hand.

"You can do this," he said quietly. They both knew they didn't have any other choice. After a moment she nodded, agreeing to go.

"Okay, everyone, stay close," Tabitha said firmly.

She ushered them into the center of the ring. As Edward stepped into it, the magical energy washed over him. It was a strange sensation, almost like being immersed in icy water. Then, just as suddenly, the feeling was gone and he found himself in a strange, new place.

The entire world had turned from color into black and white. Petrified trees, bleached white with age, stood in sharp contrast to the blackened earth. Boulders littered the hill upon which they stood, scattered around like broken teeth. The sky was dark, but there were no stars or moon. The atmosphere felt heavy.

"This place is really creepy," Edward said as he gazed around, taking it all in. Suddenly he smelled something rotten.

"Phew, what's that h-horrible smell?" he asked, wincing.

"I don't smell anything," Tabitha replied.

"Really? You can't smell that?" Edward said incredulously. "It's really b-bad! Almost as b-bad as . . ."

He suddenly remembered where he'd smelled that stench before. He'd been away from his old school for so long that he'd almost forgotten, but now the memories of the worst class he'd ever had came rushing back with horrible clarity.

Care and Maintenance of Sewer Pipes!

Edward glanced around frantically, half expecting to see his school somewhere in the immediate vicinity.

"Hey guys, look over there," Bridgette said in a shaky voice. Edward and Tabitha wheeled around to where she was pointing. A rusted archway stood behind them. On the top of the arch were words spelled out in flickering light bulbs. Edward felt a chill as he gazed at the sign. One of words was missing, the bulbs having burned out. But Edward could still make out a bit of the phrase:

. . . SPECTER . . .

And though it was an incomplete part of the name, that single word sent chills down Edward's spine. Just beyond the arch was an abandoned, broken-down carnival. It was the scariest place he'd ever seen.

A mammoth Ferris wheel towered above the silent midway. A few of its green, electric spokes flickered in the darkness, but most were burned out or missing. Beneath it, the twisted coils of a wooden roller coaster undulated like a skeletal dragon. Scattered across the rocky ground were numerous darkened booths and tents. Worst of all, the entire place seemed to be covered with pale, nearly transparent netting. At first Edward couldn't figure out why there were nets everywhere, then he suddenly realized what they were.

Webs! The entire carnival was covered with hundreds of yards of spider silk. The strands were everywhere, crossing the midway from end to end and as thick as telephone cables.

"There can't b-be any s-suh-spiders that b-big," Edward stuttered nervously.

"There can be here. In the Hollow, anything someone fears is possible," Tabitha said.

"There's no possible way I'm going in there," said Bridgette firmly. "I'd rather take my chances with the Groundlings."

"There's no going back now, only forward," Tabitha replied. "My ring will only take us in, not back out. The only way to leave this place is to face our fears."

"Well, I'm not going to do it!" Bridgette sounded hysterical. "I hate spiders. Whatever made those webs must be huge!" She quickly backed away from the imposing arch and the dark carnival beyond it. Edward noticed that one of the lengths of pale web stretched from the fairgrounds to a spot just behind her left leg. Before he had the chance to warn her, she backed into the big strand and tripped, falling backward.

The huge line trembled, sending a vibration backward, toward the carnival. As the shaking line hit the network of webs, there was a sudden whine that sounded as if someone had turned on a huge turbine engine. The three of them watched, horrified, as the Ferris wheel suddenly began to turn and a warped calliope started playing.

The deathly carnival had come to life!

And that wasn't all. There was something else moving along the surface of the webs. Bridgette screamed as she saw a long row of shapes scuttling toward them along one of the lines of webbing.

"What's that?" Edward cried.

"They know we're here," Tabitha replied softly.

"Yeah, but who's *they*?" he shouted back over the booming sound of the calliope. But before she could answer, Edward got a closer look at the row of scuttling things. At a distance he'd thought that they were spiders moving in a long row, but close-up he saw that they were something else. They were black roller coaster cars fitted with mechanical spider legs. The cars were coupled together like a train but they used their metal appendages to scuttle along the lines of spider silk.

As the cars came closer, Edward could see that this was going to be much worse than he had anticipated. Inside each of the cars was a nearly transparent being. His breath caught in his throat as he realized what he was looking at. The cars were filled with ghosts!

The passengers' tattered clothing clung to their bodies in matted rags. Their faces, some of which had once been beautiful, were now tinged a sickly shade of blue. But it was their eyes that Edward found the most disturbing. They had no irises. And every single specter's eyes were opened wide, unblinking, as if they'd witnessed unspeakable horrors.

The spider coaster was now no more than

twenty feet away. All the ghostly passengers turned their heads in unison and fixed their terrible gaze on the three of them.

"Do something!" Bridgette shouted to Tabitha.

"There's nothing we can do," Tabitha said in a defeated voice. "We have to face them. They've been sent to take us to the places we fear most."

Bridgette panicked. As the train slowed to a stop, she bolted, running away as fast as she could. The reaction from the ghostly passengers was immediate. Several phantoms shot out of the roller coaster cars, howling as they flew after her. In seconds, they had grabbed the terrified girl by the arms and hoisted her into the air.

"Bridgette!" Edward shouted. He sprinted toward the hovering phantoms, but as fast as he ran, he couldn't get to her in time. Her screams hung in the air as the phantoms carried her back toward the carnival.

Panicked, he ran back over to Tabitha, but when he got there he saw that the ghosts had her, too. The young Guardian was trapped inside one of the roller coaster cars, her wings pinned down by two Groundling ghosts. She didn't struggle, but stared straight ahead with a terrified expression. Before he could do anything to help, the train of spiderlike cars suddenly lurched forward and rocketed away, scuttling back toward the waiting carnival.

Edward's heart pounded as he stared after the retreating cars. He'd lost them both! Despair washed over him as he listened to the thundering calliope music. He had no idea why the phantoms hadn't waited to take him with them. He stood for a few minutes, stunned. Then, fearing for his friends, he began to run toward the carnival. As the massive, web-covered structures drew closer, Edward didn't know which scared him more: what had happened to Bridgette and Tabitha or whatever horrors might be waiting for him when he arrived inside.

Chapter Seventeen

THE MIDWAY

Edward marched through the carnival,
determined not to show any fear in spite of his
quaking legs. He could see many of the spider
coaster cars now, all of them containing ghostly
occupants. The cars scuttled over his head,
whisking their terrified victims to destinations
along the huge network of spiderweb cables. On
either side of him were cobwebbed booths filled
with ghostly occupants, all of whom were engaged
in terrible versions of carnival games.

A hefty ghost swung a huge hammer, trying
to ring a bell on a long pole. As the hammer
came down it suddenly changed, turning into
a python! The big man screamed as the snake
grabbed him and wrapped him in its powerful
coils.

Terrifying clowns with fangs chased a group

of young mortals through a garishly colored maze. Edward cringed as he listened to the screams echoing around him, partially drowned out by the endlessly playing calliope music. He pushed his way past several ghosts, anxiously scanning the area for any sign of his friends. He nearly bumped into a phantom that was throwing baseballs at milk bottles and trying to knock them down. But as Edward looked closer, he noticed that they weren't bottles at all. Instead, they were tiny people! They shouted insults at the ghost, urging him to try to hit them. But as many times as the ghost threw the ball, he always missed. And the more balls he threw, the more frustrated he became.

"Come on, Tony, is that all you got? You always were a weakling. What's that we used to call you? Tony, Tony, skin and boney?" said the tiny man in front.

Edward watched as the other tiny people took up the jeering chant. "Tony, Tony, skin and boney! Tony, Tony, skin and boney!"

The ghost who was Tony screamed for them to stop and threw the balls harder, but the tiny people dodged them easily, mocking every throw. The man in front kept taunting him. "Never got over losing that baseball game when you were twelve, did ya, Tony? Let down the whole team. Life would have been different if you'd have won it, but you blew the whole thing. Poor Tony. A loser in life *and* in death!"

Edward saw silver tears trickling down the ghost's face as he continued to throw, goaded on by the mocking chants. Feeling sick, Edward walked on, trying to locate his friends. Specter's Hollow really was a terrible place! He had pictured something different, perhaps a place filled with monsters. But now he understood that everyone's deepest fears were individual. For some it might be monsters, but for others there were things in themselves that they feared more than any creature.

Ghosts were all around him, but none of them seemed to pay him any attention. They were too preoccupied with their various tortures. Edward couldn't understand why the spider coaster had come for Bridgette and Tabitha but not for him. His eyes darted around the carnival as he marched on, desperately looking for any signs of his friends. Because Tabitha and Bridgette were solid, he thought that spotting them among the nearly transparent ghosts would be easy. But he was mistaken. There were so many of the howling, miserable spirits that he couldn't see them anywhere.

Edward jumped backward as a female ghost screamed next to him. She darted past as a sewer rat, as large as a horse, chased her into a sideshow tent. Edward recoiled. He hated rats. They reminded him of sewers. And he didn't care if he never saw the inside of one of those ever again.

Suddenly, as if on cue, he caught the rotten stench he'd smelled earlier. This time it was much stronger. He forced himself not to gag. Where was it coming from?

Cold fingers brushed his neck and he wheeled around. A ghost stood there with a malicious grin on his face. He was a thickset, thuggish boy with blond hair about his own age.

"G-Grudge?" Edward stammered, recognizing the face of the bully that had tormented him back at the Foundry. The stocky boy's grin widened, exposing his chipped front tooth.

"Hello, Sticks," the boy croaked, using the nickname Edward had hated. "Happy to see me?"

"Buh-buh-but h-h-how?" Edward stammered. "Are you d-d-dead?"

The phantom that looked like Grudge chuckled as if enjoying a private joke. "I've been looking for you, Bean Pole. It's time for you to wake up."

And before Edward could do anything to stop him, Grudge's meaty fist hit him on the side of the head. His legs crumpled and, as he fell, the world around him began to fade. There was one ridiculous thought that echoed again and again in his throbbing head as he lay on the ground with the calliope music thundering around him.

How could a ghost possibly hit that hard?

Chapter Eighteen
BACK TO SCHOOL

"Edward Macleod!"

The shout jolted Edward upright. He looked around, confused. He wiped a line of drool from his chin, realizing that he'd been sleeping at his desk. It wasn't possible! How could he possibly be *here?*

"Glad you decided to join us, Macleod!" said the mocking voice. Glancing up with a feeling of dread, he saw the cold, blue eyes of his least favorite teacher, Miss Polanski, boring into him through her thick, greasy spectacles. Somehow he was back at the Foundry, his terrible boarding school, sitting in the middle of his *Care and Maintenance of Sewer Pipes* class!

No! No ! NO! The smell from an exposed sewer pipe overwhelmed him. He'd smelled it since he first set foot in Specter's Hollow and now he knew why. This was the place he feared more than anything else. There was no sign of the carnival anywhere around him. He gazed back at the blue-eyed teacher with horror. *This couldn't be really happening, could it? Maybe it was just an illusion . . .*

SMACK! Miss Polanski's metal ruler smashed down, leaving a welt on the back of his wrist. He shook his hand, trying to relieve the pain. The pain was real enough to convince him that he wasn't dreaming. But if this was real, then did that mean that the Woodbine and Bridgette and Mr. Spines had all been a dream?

Not this. Anything but this! He reached his hand quickly behind him and was relieved to find that his wings were still there. At least he had those! It proved to him that he hadn't dreamed the whole thing.

Miss Polanski noticed the gesture and smirked. "If you think those things will fly you out of the sewer pipe you're mistaken. It's your turn, Macleod. Get over here and sanitize this pipe!"

Edward reluctantly stood, enduring the familiar snickers and rude comments from his classmates. This was horrible! He never thought in a million years he'd ever have to set foot in this awful place again.

At the front of the classroom, Miss Polanski handed him a length of heavy rope. His hands shook as he obediently tied it around his waist. He couldn't get over the fact that he was about to be lowered into the rotten pipe. It was far worse than any nightmare he could imagine. After the rope was secure, Miss Polanski switched on a small crane that was connected to the rope and he felt the machine slowly hoist him into the air. Then the rusty apparatus groaned as it swung him around, leaving him dangling over the fetid sewer.

Please no. Anything except this, he thought desperately. He gazed down into the darkness and filth below him, his heart racing with fear. A coarse brush and a bottle of disinfectant were shoved into his hands. The rest of the class was definitely enjoying Edward's discomfort. Someone took up a chant, crying out in a raspy voice: "Bean Pole, Bean Pole, going down the toilet hole!" It wasn't the most creative chant, but it was typical of the thickheaded students at the

Foundry. Edward glanced up and saw the brutish faces of the other boys and girls in the class, smiling stupidly and shouting the chant as loud as they possibly could.

Miss Polanski did nothing to stop it. In fact, Edward noticed that she'd even joined in herself, cackling and conducting the class with her bony finger as if it were an orchestra.

Edward struggled against the rope, trying to free himself. He prayed that something would happen, that someone would suddenly show up and put a stop to this!

Then, just as he was starting to be lowered into the pipe, the back door of the classroom burst open. Edward's head jerked up. Someone had come to rescue him just in time!

But when he saw who it was, his heart nearly stopped beating. Whiplash Scruggs, clad in his pristine white suit and plantation style hat, strode into the room. Edward felt a rush of terror greater than any he'd ever felt before. He was helpless, tied up and hanging over a sewer pipe with the person he feared more than anyone else approaching.

"Well, well, well, isn't this a revolting development?" Scruggs said, stroking his tiny, black goatee. "Seems we caught us a skinny bird that can't fly. Am I right, Miss Polanski?"

"Right you are, sir," she said, flashing Scruggs a grin with her unusually pointed teeth. Scruggs navigated his tremendous bulk through a row of desks, knocking a couple of students out of their chairs.

He drew close to the boy, a wicked smile on his fleshy face. "Mr. Macleod, you have caused me no end of trouble. Whatever shall I do with you?" Just the sound of his voice made Edward's skin crawl. Whiplash reached out a ham-sized hand and clenched Edward tightly around the back of his neck. He had a powerful grip, and Edward fought the urge to cry out as pain ran down his spine.

"Yes, my boy, more trouble than you can possibly imagine. Did you know that my master, the Jackal, has informed me that if I do not succeed this final time, I shall be . . . what was the word he used?" Scruggs paused, pretending to think. "Ah yes, I believe the word was 'obliterated.' Do you have any idea at all what that means, Mr. Macleod?"

Edward was so scared he couldn't have answered Scruggs if he tried. "It means I shall be wiped from existence. 'Unmade' as it were. You see, the Jackal is a master at destroying things. And when he destroyed the Seven Bridges, he intended that they remain that way."

He released his grip. Edward's body swayed a little on the thick rope. Scruggs bent down and opened the doctor's case he'd carried with him into the room.

"Now, it has been my experience that the best way to put a stop to a potential threat is to 'nip it in the bud' . . ." he drawled.

Edward blanched as Scruggs removed a huge pair of silver shears from the medicine bag. They were the same scissors that had plagued him in his nightmares since he'd narrowly escaped Scruggs before. He knew what two snips from them could do. His wings would be severed and he would die.

Scruggs savored the horror written on Edward's face. He rotated the big scissors in the air, examining their polished surface and gazing at them with loving appreciation. "I've been waiting for this for longer than you can imagine, Edward Macleod. You'll not get away from me this time."

Edward fought the panic that built inside of him and tried to think of a way to escape. He had to stay strong. He had to survive to save everyone else. Suddenly, he remembered something Tabitha had said: *Specter's Hollow is a place to face your deepest fears.* Up until now, he'd been too scared to think of anything but trying to escape.

But maybe that was the problem. Every ghost he'd seen at the carnival was running away from whatever it was that was frightening him or her. They'd been reacting exactly as the carnival had expected them to. He knew with sudden clarity that he had to do something different or this same scenario would keep playing itself over and over again.

He looked up at Scruggs, and tried his very best not to give in to his terror.

"Go ahead, cut 'em off!" he shouted without the slightest trace of a stutter. At Edward's words, the entire classroom suddenly fell silent. Miss Polanski gaped. Scruggs, who was still holding the scissors in the air, stared back at Edward with a stunned expression.

"You heard me," Edward continued, emboldened by his actions. "I don't care anymore. If you're here to kill me, then kill me. It doesn't matter, you know why?" Scruggs didn't answer but continued to stare at Edward, looking concerned.

"I'm not afraid of death anymore. When I lost my mother, I thought it was forever and it wasn't. Death is just the beginning. I won't let you or anyone else stop me from rescuing her now that I know that. And if death in the Afterlife means I'll be sent to Specter's Hollow, well I'm already here. I have nothing left to fear." Edward paused, allowing his words to sink in. Scruggs was looking really uncomfortable. Edward didn't know whether he was facing the real Whiplash Scruggs or if it was an illusion the carnival had produced to test him. But in the end, it really didn't matter. The effect was the same. He was standing up to the person he feared most. He'd never spoken with such authority before, and never so long without a stutter. He continued speaking, staring the evil Groundling directly in the eye.

"I'm the Bridge Builder, Scruggs. And I intend to rebuild everything your master destroyed."

Scruggs's face turned a dangerous shade of purple. He howled with rage and leaped at Edward with the scissors, ready to sever his wings.

But Edward didn't flinch. Scruggs was only an inch from his face when he and the classroom suddenly dissipated, fading away like smoke.

The next thing Edward knew, the air around him sparkled with golden light. He felt the coils of rope around his waist dissolve and his body floating to the ground. The air around him was deliciously warm, and all of the fear he'd carried since his mother died was gone. He just felt peaceful. He looked around, unable to see anything but brightness all around him. It was wonderful.

Then a gentle but powerful voice echoed around him, saying, "Well done, Bridge Builder."

Chapter Nineteen

WORKSHOP

The light faded and Edward found himself standing in the camp they had just left, next to a grove of oak trees. It was night, and a full moon bathed his surroundings in a soft, silver glow.

"Edward! You made it!"

He barely had time to register whose voice it was before Bridgette grabbed him in a fierce hug. He nearly stumbled backward under the impact.

Then, as she stepped away, he got his first good look at her. Even in the moonlight he could tell that her dress was singed and there were burn marks on her arms.

"What did they do to you?" he demanded, surprising himself with how angry he suddenly felt.

"I'm okay now," she said, forcing a smile. "But I'd rather not talk about it just yet, if that's okay," she added quietly. Edward nodded, respecting her privacy. Facing one's individual fears could be a deeply personal experience.

"Where's Tabitha?" Edward asked, changing the subject.

"Over here," the Guardian's voice came from a nearby grove of trees. She emerged, holding a skin filled with water. The Guardian's normally perfect wings looked even more disheveled than Edward's. Pearly feathers stuck out at odd angles and more than a few were bent, broken, or missing. Edward politely avoided staring at them, not wanting to embarrass her.

"I was just filling these up for the trip. There's a nice creek over there." Tabitha gazed at Edward awkwardly for a moment. When she realized that he wasn't going to ask her about what fear she'd faced, she smiled warmly up at him.

"It's good to see you made it okay, Edward." And then, to Edward's utter astonishment, she reached up and gave his shoulder a squeeze. It was the first time Tabitha had ever demonstrated that much affection since he'd met her.

"You too," he replied, smiling back.

"Hey, your stutter's gone!" Bridgette blurted, suddenly aware of Edward's lack of a speech impediment.

Edward chuckled and said, "Yeah, pretty weird, huh? I guess I left it back at Specter's Hollow."

For the first time since they'd started their journey, the three of them were able to laugh.

They decided to continue on to Melchior's workshop right away, intent on discovering the location of Cornelius's hidden valley. None of them really felt like sleeping and they knew they needed to keep moving to stay away from the Groundlings. Tabitha decided not to fly, feeling uncertain about the condition of her wings, so she rode in the back of the wagon.

They traveled in a companionable silence, nobody wanting to bring up Specter's Hollow. Tabitha preened her wings, doing the best she could to repair her feathers while Edward rode in the front next to Bridgette. The stars shone brightly overhead as the little horse plodded forward, and Edward felt that the three of them had grown much closer after experiencing such a harrowing event together.

After several hours, the trio arrived at a long, tree-lined path that led up the side of a big hill. Through the trees Edward could make out a ring of crumbling pillars at the top of it. It reminded him of a broken crown sitting on the crest of a gigantic head.

I can't believe I'm really here, Edward thought. This was where his father's story had begun. Although it had only been a few days, it seemed like an eternity since he'd sat in the cozy cottage listening to the faun tell his father's tale.

I hope Jack and the others made it to safety, Edward thought distractedly. He knew that Jack and Joyce meant the world to Bridgette. He could only hope that Scruggs and the other Groundlings hadn't been interested in them.

As they led the tired pony up the winding path to the top, he could see small globes of light flickering in the central part of the workshop.

"Is that it?" asked Bridgette.

"That's it," said Tabitha. "It's really not much to look at anymore. Jack told us that an invasion of Groundlings destroyed it shortly after Melchior fell."

Edward heard familiar voices locked in an argument as they crested the top of the hill. *Oh brother*, he thought. *They're at it again.* Back when he'd first met Sariel and Artemis they'd done nothing but argue, and, apparently, nothing had changed.

Not much remained of his father's workshop. The marble floor was cracked with shoots of grass poking up between the slabs. Broken pieces of pottery covered everything, and there wasn't a single sign of the magnificent instruments Melchior used to make. But in spite of its weathered condition, Edward had to admit that there was something inspiring about the place.

Sariel and Artemis were arguing in the middle of the room, oblivious to their newly arrived guests. Artemis, a bloated frog with green, leathery wings, was perched on a marble table shouting at Sariel, a white ermine. The ermine had her arms folded condescendingly.

"You can't tell me what to do. Melchior never said you were in charge!" Artemis shouted at her.

"He just forgot," said Sariel. "If he'd thought of it, he would have definitely said so."

Edward cleared his throat loudly. The two creatures looked up, startled.

"Edward?" Sariel said, surprised. "Thank goodness you are all right! What are you doing here?"

Then the ermine got her first glance of Tabitha, and her demeanor changed immediately. She grabbed her tail and started fiddling with it nervously. Artemis noticed Tabitha, too, and his eyes grew wide in alarm.

"Hello, Guardian," Sariel began. "I know how this must look, but we can explain our presence here. We're not Groundlings. Our master is Melchior and he instructed us . . ."

"I know your master," Tabitha said coolly. "You don't have to worry. I'm not going to turn you in to the Council."

Sariel sighed in relief. Tabitha continued, "But if you want to convince me that you aren't Groundlings, you'll need to do better than to sit there arguing about who is superior to whom."

They both looked embarrassed.

"We're sorry," Artemis said. "We haven't heard from our master in three days and we're worried."

Edward stepped forward, feeling he should be the one to deliver the bad news. "My father was captured," he said.

Sariel sat back in a stunned silence. The toad's leathery wings fluttered anxiously.

"When?" Sariel finally managed to ask.

"By who?" Artemis croaked.

"By Whiplash Scruggs. Yesterday," Edward said angrily. "And I'm not going to let him get away with it."

He gestured to the Guardian. "Tabitha has agreed to help me learn how to fly. After that, we need to find Cornelius's Valley as soon as we can. My father said that he would have the key to enter the Jackal's fortress."

Sariel nodded. "When we first returned to the Woodbine, he told us that's where he wanted to take you." She looked anxious. "But if Melchior was captured, then you'll never find it."

"Explain," Tabitha said curtly.

"The only way to Cornelius's Valley is by

using one of his magical rings to show the way. Since the ring was lost when Melchior was captured, there's no way to get there. It's too well hidden."

"My father didn't lose the ring when he was captured," Edward said.

He opened his palm, revealing his father's ring. The golden band glittered in the soft glow of the lanterns.

"How did you get it?" Sariel asked. "He would have never given it up willingly."

"He wanted me to have it," Edward said. "I guess he thought I needed to learn how to use it."

Sariel looked more concerned than ever. "I've never seen Melchior without that ring. He always said it was the most precious thing he owned."

"How do we make it lead us to where we need to go?" Edward asked.

Artemis answered, "The ring has a secret activation word. When it's spoken, the ring will lead the way. But it's a secret. Melchior never told us what it was."

Edward felt stumped. He glanced around

the shabby workplace. Could there be some clue left behind? Would his father have written the word down somewhere he thought nobody could find it? After all, if he had been in the same situation, he would have. He wouldn't have trusted his memory alone with something that important.

After gazing at several discarded crates and broken pots, Edward noticed a rack in the corner filled with small tubes that looked like they were made of stone.

"What are those?" he asked, pointing at the assorted tubes.

Sariel and Artemis both turned in the direction he'd indicated. "Those? Those are Melchior's private journals. We're not supposed to touch them."

Edward grinned. It was worth a chance.

"Well, he's my father. So I give you permission. Search through them," Edward said. "Maybe he wrote something down about Cornelius and the ring."

The two creatures looked dubious, but they obeyed. Edward was Melchior's son after all.

Bridgette offered to help, but Edward pulled Tabitha aside before she could join them, too. "I want to begin my training now, if it's okay with you," he said quietly.

Tabitha hesitated. "It's dark," she said. "Are you sure you want to learn at night? It might be harder to see the ground."

Edward glanced skyward, gazing up through the stone pillars to the twinkling stars. The night sky looked infinite, a vast empty place to stretch his ebony wings for the first time.

He gave Tabitha a determined look. "I know which direction I'm headed," he said. "And if everything goes according to plan, it won't be anywhere near the ground."

Chapter Twenty

FLIGHT

Edward balanced at a dizzying height, perched on the top of one of the stone pillars that surrounded Mr. Spines's workshop. The ground below was completely lost in shadow and he tried to keep his legs from trembling.

Don't look down, he thought, trying not to imagine what would happen if he fell to the marble floor below. Normally he would be worried that such a fall would kill him, but it wasn't death he was afraid of at the moment. The prospect of breaking every bone in his skinny body sounded really painful.

"Determine the wind direction and lean into it," Tabitha commanded. The Guardian was crouched on a nearby pillar, looking completely at ease. She had sung a Song of Lifting to get on top of the pillar.

"I c-can't," Edward stammered. And with the stutter, he felt some of his old anxiety return. His experience at Specter's Hollow evidently hadn't erased his fears completely! The boy tilted sideways and barely managed to correct himself. One false move and he was history! His heart was pounding furiously. Why had he insisted on doing this?

"Calm down," Tabitha coaxed. "Find your center."

Edward tried slowing down his rapid breathing. But it was difficult, especially when he was stranded over seventy feet in the air! *Stop fighting it*, he told himself. *Breathe!*

It didn't help. He was still terrified. In the past if he had been this anxious, he would have pulled out his playing cards and immediately commenced building a house. How he wished he had them now! Just feeling the reassuring deck in his pocket would have helped him focus.

Unbidden, images of his lost playing cards flashed through his mind. He'd played with them so often he knew each one by heart. The face cards in his deck had been unique, designed by a factory that had tried to compete with the Bicycle playing card company but had since gone out of business. He'd never seen a deck like it before or since. If he thought hard enough, he could picture each card clearly in his head.

The king of spades with his golden shovel. The jack of diamonds wearing an eye patch. The queen of hearts with her trapped peacock.

Without really thinking about it, he began assembling them in his mind, stacking one card on top of the other. His eyes lost focus as he immersed himself in the mental exercise.

Deuce of spades on top of the king, queen, and jack. Jack and eight form a tent over them. Six of hearts leans on the deuce . . .

To Tabitha, Edward seemed lost in a trance. He lowered himself a little, settling into a comfortable stance. His breathing was deep and regular. Tabitha had no idea what was happening inside Edward's mind, but the outward effect was remarkable.

"Good," she soothed. "That's just where you want to be. Now, turn your head slightly to the left. Can you feel the breeze coming from the south?"

Edward's lips barely moved as they counted the different cards running through his mind. He seemed so lost in concentration that Tabitha wasn't entirely sure he'd heard her. But then she saw his head tilt ever so slightly to the left.

The slight breeze intensified, ruffling Edward's feathers and hair. Then, without being asked, Edward shifted his position on the tall column, rotating further toward the incoming breeze. Tabitha watched him carefully, noting his every move.

"Perfect," she said. "Now comes the hard part. You've got to trust your wings. You're going to lean forward. It's going to feel very unnatural at first, but you have to get your wings into the right position so that they can allow the breeze to travel beneath them."

Tabitha knew that this was where everything could fall apart. If Edward lost faith now, he could tumble from the column. She made herself ready to sing the Song of Lifting just in case. She wished she'd brought an instrument with her. It would have amplified the magic, insuring that the Song would do its work in time. Without it, she would only have a split second to get the Song out before Edward crashed onto the marble below.

Ace of spades leans against the queen of diamonds. The queen wears her glittering tiara. The ace has a grinning skull in its center . . .

She watched as Edward leaned forward, his thin body craning itself over the edge of the pillar. In response to the wind, his wings automatically swiveled into position, creating the shape necessary to use its lifting power.

"Wait for it," Tabitha cautioned. "Feel it pull you forward."

Edward's lips continued to move. A beautiful card house of complex design had taken shape in his mind. His fingers twitched. He could practically feel the cards as he lifted them into place one by one.

Now for the last one. His mind knew exactly which of the fifty-two he'd already used. He knew every suit and value, could see every pip and pattern as if they were sitting right in front of him. There was one last card lying face down. This was the card that would go on top of his delicate construct.

He turned it over in his mind. *The joker. A laughing mime. It's eyes were alight with mischief and it wore a tasseled hat.*

Suddenly the picture on the card changed. The clown's face seemed to blur and was replaced with something else. With a start, he realized what it was. Beneath the red and black colored hat was a mangy face with yellow fangs. And he knew it immediately for what it was.

A jackal.

Suddenly Edward's eyes regained focus and he realized where he was and what he was doing. What had he been thinking? He couldn't do this. Tabitha was wrong. He was leaning too far out over the pillar! His vision swam as he saw the darkness swirling below his feet.

He tottered on the edge.

"No!" Tabitha shouted. "Stay focused!"

But it was too late. A scream tore from Edward's lips as he tumbled from the edge of the pillar, spiraling from his perch. Tabitha was so shocked that she lost the precious instant that she needed to sing in order to produce the Song of Lifting! She gazed, horrified as Edward plunged headfirst toward the stony ground.

"Pull up!" she whispered. "Pull up!"

Edward's body faded into the darkness below.

Tabitha cringed, waiting for the sickening thud that was sure to come next. The wind from the south intensified, whipping over the tops of the pillars.

Suddenly, from the shadows below, a figure soared up into the night sky. Tabitha barely caught a glimpse of Edward's thin face illuminated by the moonlight. But in that second, she saw his mouth working silently as it had when he was on top of the pillar. His mammoth, black wings were flared out dramatically on either side of him as he shot past her.

Edward was airborne!

Tabitha whooped with excitement as the thin boy's frame silhouetted against the huge moon. As he swooped and dived, her trained eye could pick out little imperfections of form. He wobbled once or twice, but whatever he was doing to keep focused was working.

Overall, she had to admit that once again

he'd surprised her. The first time had been his ability to use one of the Ten Words of Power. The second was how he'd thrown the ring with tremendous force at the Groundling outside of Woodhaven. And now, without any in-depth flying instruction, this unlikely candidate had proven that he was a natural.

Edward's antics had drawn the attention of Sariel, Artemis, and Bridgette. They were shouting words of encouragement as Edward soared, picking his way through delicate breezes.

Although he kept his mind focused on his rows of playing cards, Edward was also aware of what was happening. The cool night air flowed over and under his outstretched wings, raising goose pimples on his arms, and stinging his cheeks. His hair whipped backward, and whether it was from the forceful breezes or because of the pure joy he felt, tears flowed from his eyes and coursed down his cheeks.

He was really flying!

Chapter Twenty-One

RING

Flying was one thing, but landing was quite another. Edward tried to keep himself calm, visualizing his carefully constructed card house firmly in his mind. The wind whistled in his ears as the shadowy ground grew closer. Edward kept reciting the names of the cards to himself, forcing himself to stay calm.

Four aces on the four corners. King of diamonds, wearing his miner's cap, on the left side. Jack of hearts holding his bow and arrows, holding up the right . . .

His feet hit the ground much harder than he thought and he stumbled forward several paces. He barely missed colliding with one of the stone columns. Thankfully, he managed not to fall over and completely embarrass himself.

"Edward, that was fantastic!" Bridgette said,

rushing forward. She threw her arms around him. "You really did it! You flew!"

Edward didn't know what to say. He grinned widely and turned a deep shade of red.

Tabitha fluttered down and flashed him a smile. "That was very good. We can work on your form a little more, but overall it was an excellent first flight. Next, we'll get to work on mastering your ring and learning the Songs. You just might end up being a halfway decent Guardian, after all."

Edward beamed back at her. Although he'd had to concentrate very hard, he'd loved the sensation of soaring through the air. Once he was up there actually doing it, it had felt so natural. The muscles on his back had pushed the wings through the air and he loved the feel of his feathers as they quickly responded to the ever-changing wind currents.

"Hey, I think I found something!" Sariel's high-pitched voice called out from the rack of scrolls. Discarded tubes littered the floor around her and she had one of the scrolls unrolled in front of her.

"Is it the word?" Artemis croaked. The toad, half hopped, half fluttered to the place where the ermine sat.

"No, but it's the journal entry Melchior made right after getting the ring from Cornelius." The ermine handed the scroll to Edward, who, not wanting to read aloud, automatically gave it to Bridgette. "Y-you r-read it," he stammered.

The girl cleared her throat and read:

Thenceday, 12. W.R. 2651

Finished transaction with Cornelius. Both new rings are magnificent! C knows my plans to be with S. He's the only one I've told. The warnings I expected, but his support I didn't. He encouraged me to seek other means of achieving my goals with S. He said that, although it is unheard of, there might be a way to achieve what I want by appealing to the Higher Places.

But I told him it's too late. I've already made contact with the Jackal and made my decision. Tomorrow I fall.

Bridgette looked up from the scroll with a somber expression.

"And that's all it says," she said. She carefully rolled up the paper and replaced it in the gray tube.

Edward removed the ring from his pocket and turned it over and over with his fingers, thinking about what he'd just heard. The journal entry had mentioned two rings and Edward knew that those weren't ordinary rings. He'd seen his father wearing this one on the third finger of his left hand. There could only be one reason that Melchior had asked for two of them. They were wedding rings!

Suddenly he knew with absolute certainty how to activate the ring he held. Because there were two rings, he felt that each one of the precious bands held the other's secret word. He knew what his father would have picked. It was so obvious that he wondered why he hadn't thought of it before.

"I've got it," he said quietly. The others turned to him with expectant faces. Edward met their gaze with a small smile and said, "It could only be one thing."

He took a deep breath. The ring seemed to glimmer softly in his outstretched palm. He spoke in a clear voice, the words coming to his lips without hesitation.

"Sarah."

Chapter Twenty-Two

CORNELIUS

The wind whipped through Bridgette's hair as she clung to the space on Edward's back between his wings. Over the howl in her ears, she could pick up snatches of Tabitha's Song of Lifting, the magical melody allowing her to ride weightlessly as she held on to the skinny boy's shoulders.

She glanced in front of her to the glowing ring that hovered beyond, drawing them like a magnet to Cornelius's Valley. They had been in the air for nearly an hour and showed no signs of stopping.

Edward's massive black wings beat steadily on either side of her. Tabitha, looking like a great, impossible bird, kept pace with them. The Guardian watched Edward's movement carefully as she sang, paying attention to his form and demonstrating little corrections from time to time.

Sariel and Artemis looked right at home on Tabitha's back. It had been a long time since either of them had possessed the flying ability of a Guardian, but they clearly hadn't forgotten the feeling.

Even soaring through the air, Bridgette couldn't relax. She had been constantly worried about her honorary uncle and aunt since she'd seen their cottage on fire. She knew the terrible consequences of fires all too well. They stole away family members and left empty, burned out holes in their consuming wake.

Her mind wandered to the hospital where she hovered between life and death. If she concentrated, she could hear her father's voice, speaking softly as she lay, seemingly unreachable, in the white bed. Her poor face and body were destroyed, burned beyond recognition. And yet, her parents wanted her back, wanted their daughter to live.

"Come back to us, Bridgette. Come back, darling."

Her eyes watered, the stiff breeze carrying tears down the sides of her cheeks. She desperately wanted to see them again. But she couldn't give up on her baby sister. Somewhere up in the Higher Places, Katie was waiting for her. And the only way Bridgette could get there was if Edward could rebuild the Seven Bridges.

The ring started a downward path and Edward, at Tabitha's signal, began their descent into a fertile valley below. It was ringed on all sides by tall mountains, and would have been impossible to find from the ground.

So that's how Cornelius has managed to keep hidden from the Groundlings, Bridgette thought. Groundlings lost their ability to fly when they fell. There would have been no possible way for the evil beings to discover the spot unless someone told them exactly which mountains to climb.

A few minutes later, the ground rushed up at them. Edward made a wonderful landing. She knew he was trying to be extra careful because she was clinging to his back. She smiled.

Bridgette had often noticed the way Edward looked at her when he thought she wasn't looking. She could tell that he liked her.

She wanted to like him back, but she couldn't let herself. Although she was in the Woodbine, she was also in a coma in a hospital bed. It made her feel like she was borrowing the body she now held, the one that looked so much like she had before the accident that had robbed her of her identity.

And if he could see what I really looked like back on Earth, would he still like me?

She doubted that anyone except for her parents could love the thing she'd become. If the doctor's did help her survive, then she knew that her life from that day forward would probably be a lonely one. She couldn't allow herself to have feelings here in the Woodbine. It could all disappear and leave her heartbroken if she awoke back on Earth.

Her unhappy musing was interrupted by the slow arrival of several creatures. They were as big as houses with mammoth shells of pearly white and blue skin the color of a cloudless sky. As they moved through the tall grass, Bridgette couldn't help but be reminded of tall galleons making their way across the ocean.

When they drew closer, Bridgette got her first clear look at their faces. Their huge, human faces looked weathered but wise. When one of them spoke, it was in a deep, rich language she couldn't understand.

"SOOOOOOOOOMMM!" it bellowed, its voice causing the earth beneath her feet to tremble.

"Yes, Techote. We have guests," another, much smaller voice chimed in. It was only then that Bridgette noticed the speaker. He was an old man with a long, white beard who was riding on top of the nearest snail. He was wearing a fur cap with two curling horns extending from either side like a Buffalo.

The man climbed down a rope ladder connected to his saddle, and walked briskly over to them. For such an old man, Bridgette was surprised to see him move with such vigor.

"Welcome to the Valley of the Blue Snails," the man said, his eyes focused on the golden ring hovering above Edward's head like a halo.

"I recognize that ring. Is that you, Melchior?" the man said, beaming at Edward.

Edward didn't know what to say. "Um, no. Melchior is my father."

If the old man was shocked, he didn't show it. Instead, he smiled at Edward, revealing a mouth full of missing teeth.

"Well, bless my bones," he chuckled. "It is indeed." His smile faded and his expression grew serious.

Then, in a move that surprised them all, he removed his fur cap and bowed his wrinkled head. The two snails on either side of the old man lifted their mammoth heads skyward and gazed reverently into the heavens. Edward fidgeted awkwardly. The man bowed before him for a long moment before speaking. Then, when he finally spoke, he said something that no one, least of all Edward, expected him to say.

"Welcome, Bridge Builder," the old man said. "My name is Cornelius and it's an honor to welcome you to this valley. We've been waiting a long time for your arrival."

Chapter Twenty-Three
LAIR

It was older than the ancient trees that bordered its impregnable iron gates. And those trees were part of the Ancient Forest, a grove that went back to the earliest days, the last boundary between the lush country of the Woodbine and the desolation called the Blighted Lands.

The Jackal had built his Lair shortly after his spectacular fall, and the remnants of the Seven Bridges that he tore down with him littered the desert around his twisted palace. Some said that it was the fire from the bridges as they entered the atmosphere that created the blight, but the Jackal knew the truth. It was hate. A hate so magnificent that it blasted away any living thing in its path, leaving only bones and decay in its terrible wake.

Deep within the fortress, imprisoned in a

slime-ridden cell, was a woman dressed in tattered, blue rags. She was an important piece in a larger chess game, a white queen that every other piece on the board would soon be trying desperately to reclaim. And the Jackal waited for their attack with eager anticipation, for it meant one thing and one thing only. The boy, the son of Melchior, was bound to come for his mother. And if every other one of his best-laid plans failed, he would be waiting for Edward when he arrived. The Jackal had been searching for the boy for years and now, after such a long wait, he would force Edward to come to him. After all, how could he not? After Whiplash Scruggs's delivery of Melchior, the Jackal now possessed both of his parents. And he had a final card to play, one that would force him inside his carefully constructed web.

A high-pitched, wheezing laugh, the one that had given the Jackal his nickname, burst from his throat. A horrible, yellow eye, the Jackal's one remaining piece of living tissue, glinted with malice.

It would all be over soon. And mankind's feeble hope for a Bridge Builder would be lost for eternity.

Chapter Twenty-Four

HORSEMEN

Whiplash Scruggs hurried down the long, twisting corridor that led to the secret chamber. A pair of rusted iron keys jingled at his belt as he strode, his bulky form moving at a surprising pace for a man of his size.

He had no knowledge of Edward's encounter with the carnival's illusion of himself in Specter's Hollow. Even if he had known that Edward had taken refuge there, he wouldn't have followed. Specter's Hollow was the one place above all else that he dreaded setting foot in. Scruggs had many fears, most of which he kept secret. The thought of facing them was too terrible to imagine, because most of his fears had to do with the master he served.

Handing Melchior over to the Jackal had saved Scruggs from several terrible tortures that he would rather not think about. If he hadn't captured the traitor, he knew that his master would not have overlooked failing to capture Edward for the third time. Thankfully, it was Melchior who was being tortured instead.

Scruggs reached the end of the corridor and descended a flight of crumbling stairs. Spiderwebs clung to his massive arms as he plunged heedlessly forward, anxious to fulfill his instructions. It had been many centuries since *they* had been unleashed. They were some of the Jackal's most faithful servants, created for his use before the fall.

At the bottom of the staircase was a thick, wooden door. A grate of steel was woven over a tiny window, but looking through it revealed nothing. *They* were deep inside, shrouded in darkness blacker than the shadows.

Scruggs's hand shook as he inserted one of the big keys into the iron lock. It took considerable effort to turn and he had to throw all of his weight against the tumblers before the rusted metal finally gave way.

The door swung open with a loud, prolonged

creak. Scruggs peered into the darkness and said the words his master had instructed him to say.

"The Jackal summons you."

For a brief moment it seemed as though they hadn't heard him. Then, suddenly, there was a spark and the stench of burning oil. Four pairs of glowing eyes flared to life. The creatures' metallic flanks heaved and Scruggs hastily backed out of the doorway to allow the horsemen through. They looked like centaurs, with human torsos and horse bodies. But unlike the majestic images that most people thought of when picturing the mythical creatures, these were as horrifying as the others were beautiful.

Scruggs had seen many terrible things in the Jackal's army. But the horsemen still sent terrified shivers down his back. The first horseman was gaunt and carried a pair of rusted scales. The second was coated in rust and parts of it were crumbling with decay. The third was so big that it barely fit through the door. It carried an axe that was almost as large as Scruggs himself. But it was the fourth that made his knees weak with fear. Its skeletal head swiveled in Scruggs's direction, giving him a hollow-eyed stare that was impossible to escape. It saw *everything*.

Then, as one, they emitted a long wail. Seconds later thunder rattled through the hallway as they galloped up the stairs, anxious to follow their master's bidding.

Whiplash Scruggs had heard that once the horsemen were sent after their prey, they couldn't be stopped. The stories said that when they were unleashed, even the Jackal himself could barely control them. But Scruggs believed that his master knew what he was doing, and he hoped that, as long as he played his part and followed orders, he would remain unharmed.

"Goodbye, Edward Macleod," Scruggs whispered quietly. A fierce light shone in his piggish eyes. "You've finally been dealt cards that you cannot play."

✦ Appendix ✦

The following is a historical narrative written by Jack the faun. It is based on extensive interviews with Sariel and Artemis, and chronicles the events that led to Melchior's fall. Many scholars have debated over the document's authenticity, arguing that because Jack decided to narrate the events from Melchior and his apprentices' perspectives, it casts a shadow of conjecture on the document. However, since its publication in W.R. 2676, it has been included in the *Libram Occasum*, and has brought more attention (and much debate) about the circumstances that led to Melchior's fateful decision.

Melchior's Fall
By Jack C. Staples (Jack the faun)

A light breeze whispered through a sunny
workshop in the Woodbine, powering delicate
machines that whirred and puffed as they
worked. The brass devices had small levers shaped
like sails mounted on them that caught even the
slightest gust of wind, turning their tiny spindles
and gears with mechanical precision.

A tall, golden-winged figure stood in the
center of the room. The handsome Guardian's
gray eyes were narrowed in concentration as he
tightened the last bolt on a glittering harp. His
name was Melchior and he specialized in creating
the beautiful instruments used by all Guardians.

Melchior smiled as he replaced his wrench in a
pocket of his leather apron. The instrument had
been carved from a single mammoth diamond,
a feat that other craftsmen had thought to be
impossible.

A masterpiece! he thought proudly.

While other Guardians his age had been focused on finding mates, he had spent his time doing what he loved best. Melchior was married to his work. And although it was a lonely path, it had its rewards. He was the best craftsman that the Woodbine had seen in ten thousand years!

But I must guard against arrogance, Melchior thought grimly. He knew he was the best, but spending too much time glorying in one's accomplishments could lead to destruction. It was the same vice that had led to the Jackal's tragic fall.

Melchior took his new harp from the workbench and sat with it on a wooden stool. He placed the glittering instrument on his lap and began to play.

Instantly, a flock of transparent doves leaped from the quivering strings, taking flight as the pure notes reverberated in the open air. The handsome Guardian concentrated on each note as he sang along, his voice rising and falling with the melody. It was a Song of Renewal, and was often used by the Guardians to nurture growing things.

The song did its usual work. As the transparent birds landed in the young trees outside Melchior's window, the trees blossomed before Melchior's eyes, appearing greener and healthier as an effect of the powerful melody. Buds popped up on the branches and then beautiful flowers burst out, blooming into existence like multicolored fireworks.

As Melchior let the final note die away, he looked around to survey the results of his Song. In addition to the blooming trees, the grass was greener, the air was clearer, and everything generally looked better and healthier. A contented smile formed on his lips. Work like this never seemed like work when it brought so much joy to others.

Suddenly, a loud commotion interrupted the peace of the workshop. Melchior turned as a small Guardian burst into the room.

"Have you finished it yet, Melchior?" the boy called excitedly.

The Guardian smiled at his young apprentice and said, "Check underneath my desk, Artemis."

Melchior grinned as he watched the chubby

cherub race over to the workbench. Moments later, Artemis emerged from beneath it, holding a tightly wrapped bundle.

"Is this it?" he asked breathlessly.

"That's it! Open it up," Melchior replied.

The boy eagerly tore the silk covering away, revealing an unusually twisted, blue trumpet. The instrument had several valves at its base and two bell-shaped knobs for producing sound.

"Give it a try!" Melchior said encouragingly, his eyes twinkling. Artemis grinned and puckered up against the mouthpiece.

WOOOOONNNNNNK! The horn emitted a deep raspberry-like sound. Suddenly, something that looked a little bit like an ice cream sundae appeared on the workshop table.

"It works!" Artemis shouted.

Melchior grinned. "It's a Horn of Plenty. When played, it will produce any flavor of *manna* you like." Although it was usually eaten in it's natural, rather tasteless form, Melchior had discovered that manna, the steady diet of most Guardians, could be prepared in a variety of interesting ways. The older Guardian knew that

Artemis was especially interested in the food that human children ate. It seemed harmless to try to duplicate one of the treats he'd observed them eating down on Earth.

Artemis grinned back at Melchior and then raced to the table to try his creation. "Delicious!" he said smacking his lips in between gobs of manna, whipped cream, and a clever imitation of chocolate syrup. Then a look of mischief crossed his face. "Wait until I show Sariel that I have a magic instrument of my very own. She's going to be so jealous!"

Melchior raised an admonitory finger. "Be careful, Artemis. A Guardian shouldn't try to make others envious. Just be content and share your joy with others."

But even as Melchior instructed his apprentice, he felt like a hypocrite. Too often he'd felt the subtle corruption of arrogance sneaking into his heart about his own accomplishments.

Artemis nodded and mumbled an apology with his mouth full of manna ice cream.

Suddenly another cherub, this one a tall

girl with lavender eyes, ran into the workshop, stopping briefly to glance at her reflection in one of Melchior's shiny machines near the door. After quickly straightening her windblown hair, she walked to Melchior and said, "You'll never believe what's happened!"

"What is it, Sariel?" he asked.

The girl smiled, showing rows of dazzling, white teeth. "We've been called to the Mortal Assignment office. We're being entrusted with a human!"

Melchior's smile faded. He gazed around his workshop with a stunned expression. Being assigned as a Guardian to an Earthbound mortal was a full-time job. He would have to abandon his work!

"Are you sure there wasn't a mistake?" he asked, trying not to let his disappointment show.

"Positive!" the girl said happily.

"Hooray!" shouted Artemis. "We'll get to go down to Earth! There's so much down there I've heard about that I want to try. They've got something called licorice and, oh, bonbons and chocolate bars and blueberry pie!" The little boy's face glowed with happiness.

Melchior sighed. He hadn't counted on this. Secretly he'd thought he'd never have to leave the Woodbine, that he was too important to be called on to guard a mortal.

My own pride rearing its ugly head again, he thought miserably.

Turning to his young apprentices he said, "Well, if we must, we must. Come along, and fly in formation, please." He looked sternly at Artemis. "No acrobatics, young apprentice. Your wings aren't fully formed yet, and your weight is becoming an increasing problem."

The cherub frowned and rubbed his hand self-consciously over his round belly. Melchior took off his apron and led the apprentices to the grassy meadow outside his workshop.

"Wait for my signal," he said.

Sariel and Artemis obediently took positions next to him. Melchior unfurled his huge, golden wings. Then, after considering the wind speed and direction for a moment, he nodded to his young apprentices and said, "Wind coming in from the northeast. Watch the cross currents and

stay close to me, all right? Good. Here we go.
One . . . two . . . three!"

And with a tremendous *whooosh!* the three
Guardians shot into the air, rocketing skyward
like a flock of majestic birds.

Glittering spires rose above the golden domes
of Estrella, the Woodbine's capital city. Under
normal circumstances, Melchior would have
enjoyed looking at the beautiful architecture, but
today was different. All he could think about was
his new assignment. *This is ridiculous!* he thought.
*I have so many instruments I need to create. There
must be some mistake.*

Spotting the building he was looking for, the
Guardian alighted gracefully on a nearby "perch,"
one of the innumerable platforms designed
throughout the city for Guardian landings. Sariel
and Artemis followed, the chubby boy landing
awkwardly and almost falling off the spindly
platform.

Melchior put out a hand to steady Artemis,
giving him a disapproving look. He was usually

patient with his youngest apprentice's shortcomings, but being summoned for mortal duty had put him in a foul mood.

"You're going on a diet when we get down to Earth," Melchior said firmly. Ignoring Artemis's sputtering protests, he led them across the high bridge surrounded by cascading fountains.

They entered the beautiful dome that housed the Mortal Assignment office and Melchior walked over to the receptionist, a female Guardian wearing wire-rimmed spectacles.

"Yes?" she said brusquely.

Melchior cleared his throat and said, "I was told to report for a mortal assignment. The name's Melchior Hazshaferah."

He held his breath as the grouchy woman removed a file from a nearby cabinet. He desperately hoped she would tell him that his assignment had been a mistake. Her mauve wings twitched in agitation as she scanned the various names inside the folder. After a moment, she found the page she was looking for.

"Third floor, second hallway on your left. You'll be seeing Mr. Shofarr."

Melchior nodded crisply, trying not to look as disappointed as he felt, and motioned for his apprentices to follow.

They flew into the air, joining the crowds of businesslike Guardians that were soaring around the ceiling of the high, domed structure. On their way to the third floor, Artemis nearly crashed into an ancient-looking Guardian with gray, withered wings.

"Sorry, sir!" Artemis said, looking embarrassed.

The young Guardian shot past the flustered old man and rejoined his master and Sariel. Melchior led them down the passageway on the third floor as instructed and they soon came to a plain door with the words MORTAL ASSIGNMENT: NORTH AMERICA written on it in gold letters.

Melchior opened the door and the two apprentices followed, both of them practically bursting with excitement.

A nervous-looking Guardian with molting, brown wings and messy, light brown hair sat at a nearby desk. When they entered, he jumped, scattering a sheaf of papers on the floor.

"St. Peter's keys!" he said shakily. "You shouldn't sneak up on me like that!"

Melchior offered a curt apology. "Sorry, but the door was open." Then he added, "I'm here to report for duty."

The nervous Guardian bit his fingernail and replied in a whiny sort of voice, "Yes, yes, of course. Name?"

"Melchior Hazshaferah."

The man picked up several fallen papers, muttering, "Mickey Hashapaka . . ."

"No, it's Melchior Hazshaferah," Melchior corrected.

"Yes, yes, that's what I said. Morton Hashafrass . . ."

Melchior sighed.

After a few moments, the man found the paper he was looking for and handed it to Melchior with a feathered quill.

"Sign here, please," he said.

Melchior took the pen and glanced at the paper. The name of the mortal he was assigned to was written there in sweeping, calligraphic letters: *Sarah Macleod.*

Melchior reluctantly added his signature to the official-looking document.

The tense Guardian took the contract and moved over to a small window behind his desk. He pounded on it a couple of times until a young Guardian about Sariel and Artemis's age appeared.

"Mizrah, I need this delivered to the Records and Contracts department."

The young, freckle-faced boy took the paper and flew off at once, calling back, "Right away, Guardian Ashtooth."

Ashtooth turned back to Melchior and, after removing a large, brass key from his desk, said, "Follow me, please."

He led them across the sparsely decorated office to a heavy-looking door with iron hasps. After inserting the big key, the door swung open with loudly creaking hinges.

The younger Guardians boggled at the incredible sight before them. They had emerged inside a darkened room with a gigantic model of the Earth rotating slowly in its center.

"Amazing," Sariel whispered, staring up at

the gigantic ball. Artemis just stood with his mouth hanging open, too overcome to speak.

Ashtooth moved over to a control panel with brass switches. He bit his thumb nervously as he tried to make sense of the innumerable buttons and dials. The others watched as he scanned a huge manual, squinting at the instructions.

Finally, after several long moments, Melchior asked, "Do you need any help?"

The nervous man nodded sheepishly. "It's my first week on the job," he admitted. "And I have no idea how this thing works."

Melchior moved over to the machine and looked it over. He possessed an innate talent for all things mechanical. Within moments he discovered how the control panel operated. Turning to Guardian Ashtooth, he asked, "Where is the city I'm being assigned to?"

"Portland, Oregon, in the United States," Ashtooth replied.

Melchior pressed a few buttons and pulled down a long, walnut handle. The spinning globe in the center of the room slowed. Then, the terrain on the sphere started to change. The

North American continent swung into view and soon spread over the entire surface of the huge planet. Melchior couldn't help but be impressed by the machine as he watched the city of Portland came into focus.

"Now I need the address for, what was her name?" Melchior asked.

"Sarah Macleod," Ashtooth said. And after consulting a small leather notebook, added, "She lives on 11108 Glisan Street."

Melchior put the coordinates into the machine and a small, yellow house replaced the city view, showing a pretty woman working in a garden.

"There she is," Ashtooth said happily. "That's your mortal."

Melchior stared at the woman with an impassive expression. *So, this is the woman who is forcing me to give up all that I've worked so hard to attain.*

"She's pretty," Sariel said with a hint of jealousy.

"Yeah," Artemis added. "I wonder if she can cook."

"Rule One: A Guardian is not allowed to consume any mortal substances," Ashtooth interrupted, reading from a section marked "Rules" in his leather notebook. "Rule Two: Guardians are to remain invisible when protecting their mortals."

Artemis looked panicked. "Not consuming mortal substances" meant no Earth food! The little angel rocked back and forth anxiously. No ice cream! No bonbons! No blueberry pie! What was the point of going down to Earth if you couldn't enjoy the food?

Ashtooth continued reading, "And the third, most important rule: A Guardian is not allowed physical contact with a mortal. Failure to adhere to this rule will result in immediate termination. Do you solemnly swear to uphold these requirements?"

Melchior knew the implications of the last rule. It was a fancy way of saying that he would be cast out of the Woodbine forever if he broke it.

"Agreed," Melchior said flatly. But his two apprentices noticed the hint of bitterness in his voice.

Ashtooth marked Melchior's acceptance of the rules in his notebook.

"Your acceptance of the terms is officially noted. Now if you'll please enter transportation chambers on your left, you'll be sent down to Earth and begin your assignment immediately.

Sarah Macleod had always considered herself unlucky. But one day, for no apparent reason, that began to change. She had no idea that it was because she suddenly had a Guardian looking out for her. All Sarah knew was that, for some strange reason, things started going exceptionally well for her.

Lost keys turned up quickly. She tripped but didn't fall. The coffee table that she nearly always banged her shin against was moved a few inches to the left. Job opportunities presented themselves and generous donations from anonymous benefactors allowed Sarah to keep going.

She thought it was because she was having a stroke of luck. But Melchior and his two apprentices knew better.

Melchior was with her, watching invisibly as she woke up in the morning. He was with her as she rode the trolley to work. He watched silently as she ate her lunch, and walked beside her when she came home after a long and grueling day. He was there when she worked in her garden, nurturing her plants with her gentle hands.

And as he watched her, day after day, hour after hour, something happened to Melchior that he hadn't expected.

When he had started his new assignment, Melchior had approached it with detached professionalism. He didn't allow his personal resentment to interfere with his duty. But as time went by, and he spent every day and every night with Sarah Jane Macleod, his heart began to change. The resentment faded away. He even forgot about his workshop. He had always been alone, dedicated to his work more than anyone or anything else. But now he felt something he'd never known.

He'd fallen in love.

He'd grown to love the way Sarah looked in the morning sunlight. He loved the way she put exactly two teaspoons of cream in her tea. He loved the way she tucked her hair behind her ears when she was thinking. But most of all, he loved watching her hands as they worked in her garden. She handled her plants with the same nurturing touch that he used when he crafted his instruments.

And he wanted those hands to touch him more than anything else he'd ever wanted in his life.

He pined away daily for the mortal woman, feeling frustrated that she couldn't see the little ways he constantly looked out for her. He envied the comb that got to touch her auburn hair. He was jealous of the pillow that caressed her sleeping cheek. He was consumed with his love for her. And after weeks of longing, he decided to do something desperate. He couldn't live another moment without introducing himself to Sarah Macleod as her secret admirer and protector. There was only one choice left and he knew it would change his life forever.

He decided to fall.

Coming Soon:

THE MYSTERIOUS MR. SPINES

SONG

RECKONING

A blistering wind blew over the sea of yellow grass. Four shadows, dark against the brilliant blue horizon, cantered to a stop. Bones, the leader of the mechanical centaurs turned his face to the wind and inhaled. There was a slight whistle as the air filled the holes where his nostrils should have been. There was a pause. Then he pulled his hat lower, casting a shadow on his skeletal features.

"Macleod," he hissed. The horseman turned, maneuvering the bottom half of his equine body to face his comrades. The other centaurs were no less horrifying than their leader. But there was no mistake as to who was in charge. They obeyed him, for his unique power enabled him to end any argument and lay to permanent rest any usurper.

Blades, the biggest of the other three centaurs, had the lower half of a plow horse and the upper body of a battle-scarred warrior. He was dressed in scarlet and wore a huge, pitted axe at his belt. "How far is he from here?" he demanded in a flat, electronic voice.

"Two nights, maybe three," replied the skeleton.

"We have him now," whispered the third horseman. Blight was dressed in rags, and very thin. Her eyes blazed with an unhealthy light and her filament hair whipped in the breeze like a tattered flag.

"None escape the Four," agreed Bugs, the fourth centaur. He was lumpy and misshapen, his face a mass of twisted metal and rusted parts. His single, electronic eye surveyed the beautiful countryside and his mechanical brain clicked with possibilities. Pestilence and plague followed wherever he went and he delighted in the prospect of more beauty to ravage.

After a signal from the skeleton, the Four turned as one and set off behind their leader. The pounding of their iron hooves caused huge clouds of dust to billow after them as they thundered across the broad valley.

Edward Macleod had no idea what was coming. And even if he had, there wouldn't have been much he could do to stop them. They were the Four. And since time began, they had never been defeated.

HEAVENLY WINGS

The icy wind stung Edward's cheeks as he flew higher and higher. He was pushing himself, trying for an altitude he'd never attempted before. He glanced to his left and right, watching as his long, black wings pushed through the wind, forcing their way effortlessly through the powerful currents.

He felt strong. And this was a new feeling for him. Until recently he'd been nothing but a gangly, insecure fourteen-year-old with a terrible stutter. But now, as he soared above the clouds, gazing down on the green valley below, he felt like that part of him was long gone. It was no accident that he'd sprouted wings. He was a Guardian, a protector of mortals. And here in the Afterlife, he was at home.

The ground below was in miniature. He

gazed down through the clouds and could see the peaks of tiny mountains. If he squinted, he could just make out a string of tepee-styled huts next to them. From this height, they looked like a row of thimbles.

Edward smiled. It was Cornelius's Valley of the Blue Snails, a secret place that most of the Afterlife residents didn't believe existed. But Edward had found it with the help of his father's ring.

If only he was here and could see me now, Edward thought wistfully. His father, Melchior, would have been proud to see how accomplished at flying Edward had become. After all, his father had been an important Guardian once, long before the fall that had stripped him of everything, including his wings.

It had been a tremendous sacrifice. But Edward's father had done it to be with Edward's mother, a mortal, and had been willing to pay any price. And pay he did—making a deal with the Jackal to join his evil army in exchange for Edward's mother's hand. But all along, Edward's father had a secret plan. When the time had come for him to fulfill his end of the contract and join the army, Edward's father ran away with his wife and newborn son and hid, hoping to escape the Jackal's notice.

But there was no way to outrun the Jackal's Corruption. It was a disease used by the Jackal to convert fallen Guardians into warped, twisted creatures that served only him. The disease had transformed his father from his once handsome form into a shrunken, spiny creature. Worse, there was a hidden clause in the contract that resulted in Edward's mother's untimely death. Melchior should have known that trying to outsmart the Jackal had been foolish, but he'd been blinded by his love for Edward's mother, and his arrogance had been his downfall.

And that was why, after he had unexpectedly sprouted wings at his boarding school in Portland, Oregon, Edward had found his way to the Afterlife. He'd learned that after his mother had died, she had become a prisoner in the Jackal's Lair. And even though everyone here in the Woodbine told him that it was impossible, he was determined to rescue her from the Jackal's clutches.

It was getting cold. Edward's back ached from flying so high and he noticed little ice crystals shining on his ebony feathers. He knew that he'd reached his limit and wouldn't be able to keep climbing much longer. Preparing himself for the long glide back down, and anticipating the wonderful feeling of riding the air currents, he turned his gray eyes away from the infinite heavens. Gliding was much less work than forcing himself against the wind.

As his long body drew a graceful arc in the air and turned downward, he spotted a glittering speck on the horizon. At this distance, he couldn't tell if it was a bird or a Guardian.

Maybe it's Tabitha! His Guardian friend flew better than anyone in the Woodbine. Wouldn't she be impressed to see how high he was! Edward flapped toward the speck, eagerly anticipating the meeting.

As he drew closer, his powerful wings suddenly faltered.

Rolling, black clouds filled the sky behind the other flier, punctuated with intermittent flashes of lightning. Turbulence caused his wings to lose their lift. His stomach flip-flopped as he struggled to maintain his course.

But the approaching figure seemed undeterred by the storm. As it grew larger, Edward could tell that it was moving through the buffeting winds with greater ease than he was. He could see now that it wasn't Tabitha. Whoever it was, was a much larger and more powerful being. For a moment, Edward thought that it must be Jemial, the huge Guardian warrior he'd met shortly after he'd arrived in the Woodbine.

But then a flash of lightning reflected off the shiny object the figure held. Edward gasped, realizing what it was. A chill deeper and more penetrating than the icy winds he'd been fighting filled his bones. Grasped in the powerful figure's hand was a pair of long, bladed scissors, a weapon carried by the one person Edward dreaded more than any other. It was Whiplash Scruggs, the Jackal's most fearsome commander. And Edward knew, with a terrible, sickening feeling, exactly why he was carrying the silver shears.

Edward tried to turn back. But the wind

was howling all around him and the storm was closer than ever, making any maneuver difficult. He strained against the turbulent air, pushing himself as hard as he could against the forceful gale. His wings were battered by the heavy wind, slowing his progress to a painful crawl. His heart hammered in his chest. He had to get away!

He glanced behind him and saw, to his horror, that his bulky enemy was now directly behind him. He could see the man's piggish features clearly now. Scruggs's pointed teeth were bared in an animal snarl and his piercing, blue eyes bore into Edward's own with hungry anticipation.

Suddenly, he felt a hand close around his ankle. Then the voice he dreaded more than any other shouted in a terribly familiar Kentucky accent, "You're mine, Bridge Builder!"